Qin
Dragon Emperor of China

Chronicles of the Watchers
Book 2

By Brian Godawa
Story by Charlie Wen & Brian Godawa

Previously titled *The Dragon King: First Emperor of China*
Chronicles of the Watchers Book 1

Qin: Dragon Emperor Of China
Chronicles of the Watchers Book 2
3b Edition

Original title: The Dragon King: First Emperor of China

Warrior Poet Publishing
www.warriorpoetpublishing.com

ISBN: 9798711100812 (hardcover)
ISBN: 978-1-942858-55-3 (paperback)
ISBN: 978-1-942858-54-6 (ebook)

Get a Free eBooklet of the Biblical & Historical Research Behind This Novel.

Limited Time Offer

FREE

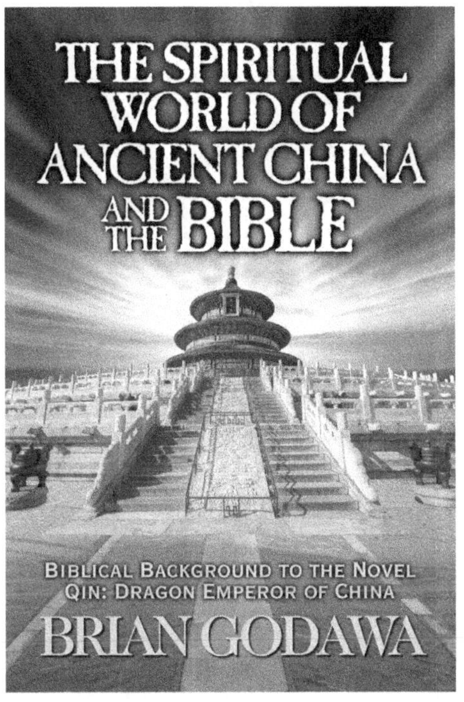

Explore the Spiritual World of the Ancient Land.

If you like the novel *Qin*, you'll love discovering the biblical and historical basis for the fascinating, mind-bending story.

Go to page 242 to see how to get the FREE eBook.

Also available for purchase in paperback.

ACKNOWLEDGMENTS

Special thanks to our wives, Kimberly and Lika, our goodly queens of love, support and treasure above gold. And to Michael Gavlak, for his helpful story scrutiny. And to Sarah Beach, our editor.

NOTE TO THE READER

This novel was previously published with the title: *The Dragon King: First Emperor of China*. The text remains the same. Only the title and cover have been changed.

I receive commissions on all links to Amazon books in this book.

Qin: Dragon Emperor of China is a standalone novel. But it is a part of the *Chronicles of the Watchers* series whose books all share what biblical scholar Michael S. Heiser has coined "the Deuteronomy 32 worldview."[1]

Rather than try to re-explain this worldview within the story of each novel, I will lay it out here in brief summary. For more detailed biblical support and explanation, I recommend reading my booklet, *Psalm 82: The Divine Council of the Gods, the Judgment of the Watchers and the Inheritance of the Nations (paid link)*. It is the foundation of all three of my novel series, *Chronicles of the Nephilim, Chronicles of the Watchers* and *Chronicles of the Apocalypse*.

Deuteronomy 32 is well-known as the Song of Moses. In it, Moses sings of the story of Israel and how she had come to be God's chosen

---

[1] Michael S. Heiser, *The Unseen Realm: Recovering the Supernatural Worldview of the Bible*, First Edition (Bellingham, WA: Lexham Press, 2015), 113–114.

nation. He begins by glorifying God and then telling them to "remember the days of old"…

> When the Most High gave to the nations their inheritance,
>   when he divided mankind,
> he fixed the borders of the peoples
>   according to the number of the sons of God.
> But the Lord's portion is his people,
>   Jacob his allotted heritage.
> (Deuteronomy 32:8–9)

The context of this passage is the Tower of Babel incident in Genesis 11 when mankind was divided. Rebellious humanity sought divinity in unified rebellion, so God separated them by confusing their tongues, which divided them into the seventy nations (of Gentiles) described in Genesis 10, and their ownership of those bordered lands as the allotted "inheritance" of those peoples.

But inheritance works in heaven as it is on earth. For the people of Jacob (Israel) would become Yahweh's allotted inheritance, and the other Gentile nations were the allotted inheritance of the *Sons of God*.

So, who were these Sons of God who ruled over the Gentile nations (Psa 82:1-8)? Some believe they were human rulers, others argue for their identities as supernatural principalities and powers. I am in the second camp. In my *Psalm 82* book, I prove biblically why they cannot be humans and must be heavenly creatures.

The phrase "Sons of God" is a technical term that means divine beings from God's heavenly throne court (Job 1:6; 38:7) and they are referred to with many different titles. They are sometimes called "heavenly host" (Isa 24:21-22; Deut 4:19 with Deut 32:8-9; 1 King 22:19-23), sometimes called "holy ones" (Deut 33:2-3; Psa 89:5-7; Heb 2:2), sometimes called "the divine council" (Psa 82:1; 89:5-7), sometimes called "Watchers" (Daniel 4:13, 17, 23) and sometimes called "gods" or *elohim* in the Hebrew (Deut 32: 17, 43; Psa 82:1; 58:1-2). Yes, you read that last one correctly. God's Word calls these beings *gods*.

But fear not. That isn't polytheism. The word "god" in this sense is a synonym for "heavenly being" or "divine being" whose realm is that of the spiritual.[2] It does not mean uncreated beings that are all-powerful and all-knowing. Yahweh alone is that God. Yahweh is the God of gods (Deut 10:17; Psa 136:2). He created the other *elohim* ("gods"). These "gods" are created angelic beings who are most precisely referred to as Sons of God.

The biblical narrative is this: The Fall in the Garden is not the only source of evil in the world according to the Bible. Before the Flood, some of these heavenly Sons of God rebelled against Yahweh and left their divine dwelling to come to earth (Jude 6), where they violated Yahweh's holy separation and mated with human women (Gen 6:1-4). This was not a racial separation, but a spiritual one. Their corrupt hybrid seed were called "nephilim" (giants), and their effect on humanity included such corruption and violence on the earth that Yahweh sent

---

[2] Michael S. Heiser, *The Unseen Realm: Recovering the Supernatural Worldview of the Bible*, First Edition (Bellingham, WA: Lexham Press, 2015), 23-27.

the Flood to wipe everyone out and start over again with Noah and his family.

Unfortunately, after the Flood, humanity once again united in evil while building the Tower of Babel, a symbol of idolatrous worship of false gods. So, Yahweh confused their tongues and divided them into the seventy nations. Since man would not stop worshipping false gods, the living God gave them over to their lusts (Rom 1:24, 26, 28) and placed them under the authority of the fallen Sons of God that they worshipped. Fallen spiritual rulers for fallen humanity (Psa 82:1-7). It's as if God said to humanity, "Okay, if you refuse to stop worshipping false gods, then I will give you over to them and see how you like them ruling over you."

This incident of the Tower of Babel comes into play in the story of *Qin: Dragon Emperor of China*. But I will let the novel reveal how.

Deuteronomy 32 hints at a spiritual reality behind the false gods of the nations, calling them "demons" (Deut 32:17; Psa 106:37-38). The Apostle Paul later ascribes demonic reality to pagan gods as well (1 Cor 10:20; 8:4-6). The New Testament continues this ancient notion that spiritual principalities and powers lay behind earthly powers (Eph 6:12; 3:10). The two were inextricably linked in historic events. As Jesus indicated, whatever happened in heaven, also happened on earth (Matt 6:10). Earthly kingdoms in conflict are intimately connected to heavenly powers in conflict (Dan 10:12-13, 20-21; 2Kgs 6:17; Judges 5:19-20).

So the Bible says that there is demonic reality to false gods. Just what this looks like is not exactly explained in the text of Scripture. But since those Sons of God who were territorial authorities over the nations were spiritually fallen Watchers, that makes them demonic or evil in essence. So what if they were the actual spiritual beings behind the false gods of the ancient world? What if the fallen Sons of God were masquerading as the gods of the nations in order to keep humanity enslaved in idolatry to their authority? That would affirm the biblical stories of earthly events with heavenly events occurring in synchronization.

Psalm 82:8 hints at the final judgment of these fallen gods, when it links their disinheritance of the nations to Yahweh "arising" and inheriting the nations from them. He will literally take back their territorial rights and power. The messianic connection is obvious and explained in more detail in my book, *Psalm 82*.

That is the biblical premise of the *Chronicles of the Watchers Series*. The pagan gods, like Yu Huang, the Three Pure Ones and others, are actually fallen Sons of God, Watchers of the nations, crafting false identities and narratives as gods of those nations. The ultimate end of these spiritual rebels is depicted in the series, *Chronicles of the Apocalypse (paid link)*. But for now, they plan, conspire and fight to keep their allotted peoples and lands, all while seeking to stop God's messianic goal of inheriting all the nations (Psalm 2:1-9; 82:8).

PRONUNCIATION OF WORDS

Translation of Chinese into English pronunciation is a difficult thing. The modern standard established during the 1950s is called pinyin. But for Western English readers, pinyin is problematic because key consonant sounds are not the same as we read them. Since the language of most of my current readers is English, I have provided a table for pronunciation of the Chinese words used in this novel. I have made several exceptions to this rule. First, I have translated the family name of Qin into the older Wade-Giles standard of Ch'in because it illustrates the obvious influence of that name upon the later Chinese culture as a whole. I have also translated Li Si's name into the Wade-Giles standard, Li Ssu, because of its more intuitive rendering for English readers.

Chinese Pinyin	English Pronunciation
Shang Di	Shong Dee
Li Si (Li Ssu)	Lee Soo
Qin Shi Huang Di (Ch'in Shih Huang Di)	Chin Shuh Hwong Dee
Fusu	Foo Soo
Huhai	Hoo High
Mei Li	May Lee
Meng Tian	Meng Tee-en
Xu Fu	Zoo Foo
Fan Zhou	Fahn Joe
Xiongnu	Shawng-noo
Langya	Lang-yeh
Xianyang	Shee-an-yahng
Xian	Shee-an
Yanjing	Yan-jing
Tianxia	Tien-shee-uh
Juren	Joo-ren
Zhen Li	Jen Lee
Yu Huang	Yoo Hwang

Greek words	English Pronunciation
Magi	May-j eye
Magus	May-guss
Xeneotas	Zen-ee-uh-tuss
Antiochus	An-tie-uh-cuss
Seleucia	Si-loo-shuh
Seleucid	Si-loo-sid

MAP

Land of the Barbarians
(Xiongnu)
THE LONG WALL
THE LONG WALL
Yanjing
Bo Hai
Langya
Yellow
Sea
Wei River
Xianyang
Emperor's Tomb
Ch'in Empire
Tianxia
East
Sea
Boundary
of Ch'in Empire
(Continues with the Great Wall)
N
South
Sea
200 miles

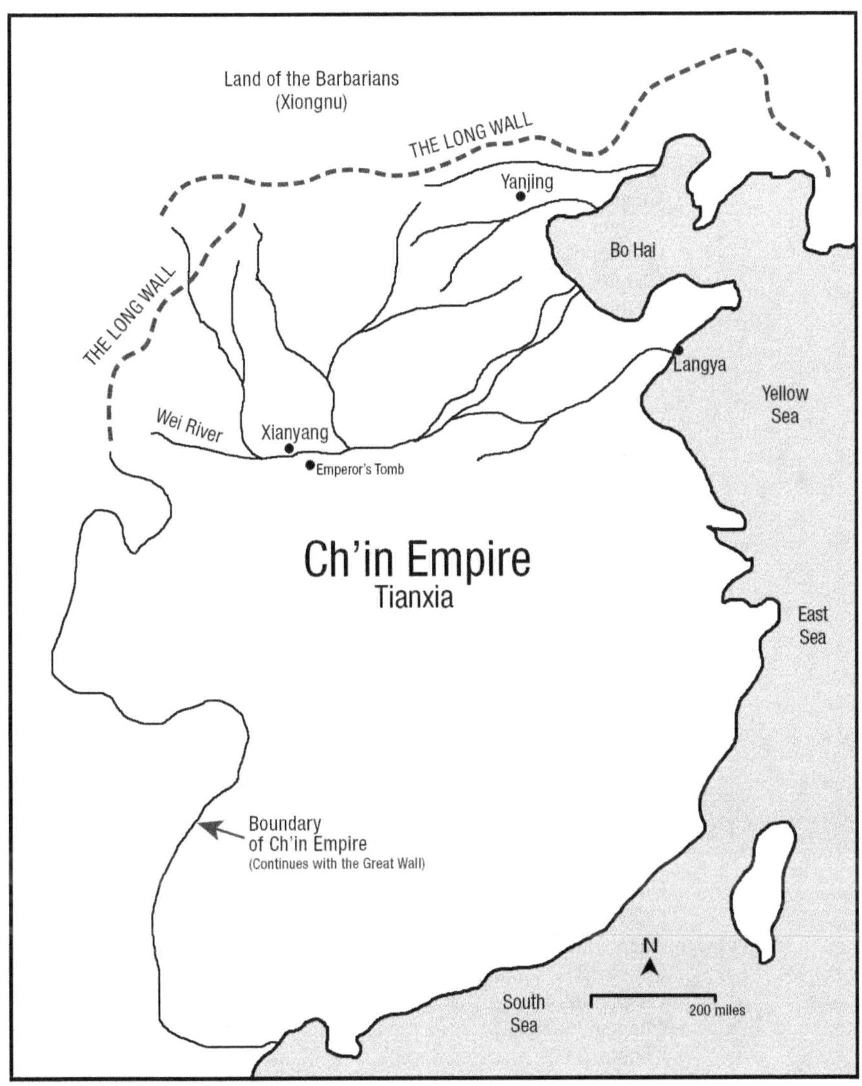

TABLE OF CONTENTS

CHAPTER 1

Year 90 A.G., *Anno Graecorum*, year of the Greeks. (221 B.C.)

Xeneotas stood at attention in the throne room of King Antiochus the Great, in the capital city of Seleucia on the Tigris, in Mesopotamia. At twenty-three years of age, Xeneotas was the youngest general in the armed forces of the king. He had achieved high honor for his fighting skills and battlefield leadership in the military academy. His flowing raven-black hair, dark eyes, high cheek bones and muscular build left his peers with an imposing impression of mystery. He lacked the hairiness of his Greek counterparts, which made him seem superior though alien.

He now stood in line with other generals amidst a grand wedding display in the crowded, pillared throne room. He watched the king sitting on his golden throne at the front of it all, elevated above them.

The monarch rubbed his gray-haired temples from an apparent headache, careful not to remove the diadem, a royal cloth band knotted around his head that distinguished him as sovereign. As all kings before him, he was clean shaven in imitation of Alexander the Great. Most of the military followed this same fashion. He adjusted the regal purple robe that crumpled uncomfortably beneath him, and fiddled with the royal gem-studded scepter, another Greek royal symbol since the days of the *Iliad*.

Antiochus looked tired, crestfallen, and Xeneotas knew why. The king was marrying the beautiful Laodice III of Pontus, his maternal cousin. Royal courtiers in expensive wedding garb surrounded his throne before the sea of aristocratic observers in the long walkway to the throne. It was glorious and celebratory, but Xeneotas knew it was not what the king really wanted.

Perhaps it was a life of suspicion that tired the great ruler more than anything else. When you governed an expanding kingdom of such size, the number of those who sought to wrest power from you was equally expanding. His kingdom included northern Mesopotamia and stretched all the way from Anatolia in the west to Media and Parthia in the east. Some one million square miles of territory with over fifteen million subjects.

The Seleucid dynasty had begun over a hundred years earlier with the death of Alexander the Great. Civil wars for power immediately followed until the kingdom was divided between four of his previous generals, the *Diadochi*, or "The Successors." Seleucus, the forefather of Antiochus was one of them. The others were Ptolemy, Antigonus and Attalus. Eventually, the Seleucid empire dominated the northern and eastern regions, and the Ptolemies dominated the west and the south of Egypt. The Antigonids ruled Macedonia. The republics of Rome and Carthage loomed on the horizon as a shadow of increasing danger. But for now, the Seleucid kingdom's greatest concern was with the expanding reach of the Ptolemies into the land of Palestine. This marriage to Laodice would create diplomatic ties with Pontus in the north, and with it, an ally against the encroaching Ptolemaic interests from the south.

Power could not be achieved or maintained without politics.

The king's most trusted advisor and prime minister, Hermias, stood beside him like a bird of prey on the arm of a falconer. This grizzled war veteran and ruthless advisor had recently forced another general, Epigenes, into retirement. They had given contrasting advice to the king regarding the rebel Molon, governor general of Media. Molon was leading a revolt against Antiochus. Epigenes had counseled the king to inspire his forces by personally leading them in battle against Molon. Hermias counseled the king to stay out of the fight, and lead from a safe distance. His life was too valuable to risk out on the field of battle. But because the treasury was so low, Hermias promised to personally pay for the battle, if the king led from behind the forces, and Epigenes retired to his home town. Antiochus followed the former's advice. Hermias was a brilliant strategist on and off the battlefield.

As protective as Hermias appeared to be, Xeneotas knew he still sought personal gain. But his loyalty to the throne had been consistent. His war-scarred body and face illustrated his willingness to die for the Seleucid cause. Xeneotas knew the king respected Hermias for his ability to maneuver his personal interests in subjection to his support for the crown. All men sought power. Those who pretended not to were the ones most suspicious to the king. Xeneotas didn't trust any of the generals.

But then again, Xeneotas wasn't exactly the most trustworthy of subjects either. He had a secret of his own. Something he wanted to prove to the king.

The musicians began playing flute, lyre, and harp, as all eyes turned to look for the arriving queen-in-waiting. But Xeneotas kept his gaze upon the king, who now stood to receive his bride. Xeneotas looked with envy upon the man that he felt he knew better than the sycophants and plotters around him did. He could see the pain in the king's eyes. Though the people treated their kings as gods, Xeneotas knew Antiochus was very human.

Previous Seleucid kings had taken epithets to distinguish themselves with increasing self-aggrandizement. The first Seleucus dubbed himself Seleucus Victor. His son called himself Antiochus Savior. His son became Antiochus God. Antiochus the Great took his title from Alexander, his more human, yet no less imperious, example of power and vainglory.

But Xeneotas knew the king's secret. He knew why this man could never be satisfied with all the power in the world.

Antiochus the king stared down the long, pillared approach to the throne. The future queen now stood in the entrance, dressed in dazzling display of the finest Greek adornment. A white dress, augmented by gold and turquoise jewelry. Mediterranean cosmetics on perfectly pale skin made soft with honey and perfumed with herbal ointments. A translucent veil covered her braided hair, her darkened eyes, enticing. She was a goddess. She glided slowly past the crowd on her way to the throne where king and priest stood waiting to officiate the holy matrimony.

Yet, Antiochus did not see her. His thoughts drifted away to the painful memories of his haunted past. This woman, Laodice, this royal queen-to-be, was a politically important alliance, she was even a spectacle of poise and beauty.

But she was not Thera.

All he wanted to see was Thera. All he would never see was Thera. The only treasure he coveted in all his kingdom of power and glory were the fading memories of his youth, of a sixteen-year old servant with a mixed foreign ancestry, the only woman he had ever loved.

Antiochus had noticed Thera because she stood out from the plethora of servants in the palace. He was admittedly drawn to her exotic look. Rich black hair, almond eyes, alabaster skin. But even her ways were different from any he had known. Centuries of imperial expansion and the overthrow of kingdoms brought with it an intermixing of all kinds of unusual foreign slaves and subjects. Some kept their cultures, many assimilated. Thera's family veiled theirs.

But she had told Antiochus her secret name, a memory of her people. She was called Zhen Li by her parents, which meant "truth." He had kept his vow to never reveal her truth to anyone. It was the only vow he had ever kept. Along with the only memories he cherished. In return, he gave her his princely signet ring with the king's seal on it. She could show it to no one, for he did not have the authority to do such a thing.

Young, innocent, forbidden love. Stealing away with every opportunity. They pledged their bodies and souls to one another.

Antiochus felt a rising dread within as his memories of her soft skin faded away. He had difficulty remembering the wetness of her lips and the silkiness of her hair. The sweetness of her breath, the musty perfume of her scented neck, her dark and mysterious eyes of beauty were all dissolving in the mists of the past.

The strongest memory that haunted his cloudy, aging mind was the shocking, intrusive pain of their discovery. Of the king's guard pulling them apart, never to see or touch one another again. Of his signet ring, hidden in her hand as his only capable act of defiance before submitting to the inevitable. Of her secretly kissing the gold ring with eyes pouring out rivers of pain. They could never be man and wife. She was nothing. He would be king.

But the fading fog of that ghost was overtaken by the flesh and blood bride that now stood before Antiochus, reaching to grab his hand. They turned to the magus priest who would marry them before the gods.

•••••

Xeneotas stood drinking with the magus Balthazar in the afterhours banquet of celebration. Balthazar was the son of the high priest of Marduk in the temple of Babylon. Magus meant "wise man." The priesthood of magi had a long history in Babylon and provided the power of magic and wisdom for the king. Magic and wisdom from both sages and the gods.

Balthazar was the same age as Xeneotas, but unlike his comrade, Balthazar rejected power and glory. He had inherited the high priesthood, but had scandalously turned it down. It never made sense to Xeneotas, as so little of the esoteric priest did.

They were surrounded by the loud celebration of royalty and aristocracy. Dancing women, flowing beer and wine, roasted boar, pheasant and gazelle.

"Now is not the time," said Balthazar. "The king is newly married. Give it some time."

"I can wait no longer," said Xeneotas.

A servant approached them with a platter of honey cakes. They turned her away.

"Xeneotas, am I not your trusted friend?"

Xeneotas would not respond. He knew the other was drawing him into a trap.

"Am I not a magus?"

"The gods have never been of much wisdom to me, Balthazar, you know that."

"At least then, grant me the wisdom of the sages."

Xeneotas could not hold back his smile.

Balthazar continued, "And they are in concurrence with the stars and the gods. Do not do this. You will lose everything you have worked so hard to gain."

"I am sorry, my friend," said Xeneotas, "I no longer care. I have nothing else to lose."

"My generals!" The voice of the king drew their attention. From their scattered locations in the hall, the generals gathered about the king. Xeneotas saw a winded messenger with the king.

Hermias stared at Xeneotas as the king spoke. "Molon advances upon Babylon." Balthazar lost his breath. Babylon was his home and the location of his holy temple. It was a mere ten miles southwest of where they were now in Seleucia.

After a moment of reflection, the king concluded, "Xeneotas, I want you to be the chief commander. Assemble a regiment to defend the city and capture this rebel."

"Yes, my lord."

The king added, "Use the sorcery of the magi to augment your forces." Xeneotas exchanged glances with Balthazar. They would fight beside one another.

This was the moment for Xeneotas. This was his chance to garner respect with a crushing victory that would finally grant him a special audience with the king and allow him to share his secret.

He would gather his forces and leave for the ancient city immediately.

CHAPTER 2

Xeneotas and Balthazar stood on the parapet of the north fortress and looked out over the Euphrates river that ran through the middle of the great city, Babylon. The *once great* city. Behind her towering walls of brick lay the streets, towers and temples of fading glory. Her hanging gardens, once a splendorous wonder of trees and plants adorning a vast garden complex for the gods, were now gone. Dried up and dead in the heat of the Mesopotamian sun. The huge temple complex housed the ziggurats named Etemenanki and Esagila, step-pyramids that rose to the heavens, now crumbling and in disrepair. They were still used by the magi priests for their services on behalf of the king and his kingdom, but woefully unfunded and rarely visited by the diminished population within the walls.

When her conqueror, Alexander, died a hundred years earlier, Babylon was caught in the middle of the fight for control between the four Diadochi. She had suffered much damage from which she never recovered. Most of her residents had been moved up to Seleucia. But sacrifices were still offered in her holy places by the magi who kept them up with a sacred calling.

Xeneotas and Balthazar were joined by their captains just above the Ishtar Gate, famous for its glorious display of blue and gold-accented brick. Its gateway walls were covered with large mosaics of lions, bulls and mushussu, which were hybrid creatures of part dragon, part feline and part eagle.

In the distance, several miles away, they could see the encampment of the rebel general Molon.

"How many troops do you think he has?" asked Balthazar.

"Five thousand," said Xeneotas.

"How many have we mustered?"

"Four thousand. But the numbers are not what concerns me. Molon's cavalry does."

As satrap governor of Media, Molon had the benefit of a sophisticated economy of horse breeding. Thus, his warriors were unbeatable on horseback. He was joined in this revolt by his brother Alexander, the satrap of Persia, and his infamous warrior cult, the Immortals. Together they represented the two most important eastern provinces for Seleucid rule.

Xeneotas said, "I have warned Hermias too many times that the king is overextended in his ambitions. He should have waited to build up his security forces for occupation before he launched into his expansion in the east."

Balthazar mused, "What measure of power will satisfy a man?"

"Just a little more," said Xeneotas.

Balthazar nodded in sad agreement.

They saw a messenger arrive on horseback from Seleucia. Balthazar said, "The divination report."

Babylonian magi regularly consulted their celestial omen texts, such as the *Enuma Anu Enlil*, in order to divine the signs for the king. He could then make civil or military decisions based on the good or bad omens divined on his behalf.

Xeneotas stared out at Molon's distant forces, as Balthazar received the royal communiqué and read silently from the scroll.

Xeneotas spoke to his watching captains, "They are on the move. Mount up and ready our forces outside the walls."

"No," interrupted Balthazar. He held up the scroll. "The king orders us not to ride out, but to retreat behind the walls, and perform a sacrifice to the gods. The stars predict disaster outside the walls."

The captains looked to Xeneotas for orders. He remained staring out in the distance. He muttered, "Gods and stars. Superstition. Prepare your magic, Balthazar."

Balthazar leaned close to his friend so as not to be heard by the officers. "Xeneotas, you have known my loyalty since we were children. Do not do this."

Xeneotas hissed back, "I can crush this rebellion now. Save the kingdom. Earn the honor of my—king." His hesitation was not obvious to the captains. But it was to Balthazar.

"You cannot achieve the king's tribute by disobeying his orders."

Xeneotas said dryly, "I never received his orders." He looked at one of the captains. "Imprison the messenger and burn the scroll." He looked at Balthazar who reluctantly handed the captain the scroll.

Xeneotas reiterated, "Prepare your magic."

Xeneotas' army lined up on foot and horseback over the western banks of the Euphrates river. A garrison of Greek citizen soldiers called hoplites wore light battle skirts, shin greaves, menacing Phrygian helmets and bronze breastplates. They carried short swords, shields and long spears. They lined up in phalanx position as a wall of impenetrable bronze, iron and muscle.

Molon and three thousand of his men faced them across a divide of several hundred yards of desert plain. Xeneotas could see that Molon had only garnered five hundred or so of his infamous cavalry with their "chopper" swords on their purebred warhorses. A chopper sword was extra large for an increased span of attack by the horsemen. They looked like dragon's teeth.

So, this rebel is overly confident, thought Xeneotas. *He thinks he needs a mere five hundred. His presumption is my advantage.* He glanced over his shoulder at the line of a dozen catapults wheeled out behind them. He turned to Balthazar and nodded.

Balthazar raised his standard. As a magi warrior, his dress was significantly different from the others. He wore all black leather as his armor. It was not as protective as bronze, but it was much lighter and afforded him the freedom to move more fluidly than his enemies. Even his helmet was a leather fitted mask more apropos for a sorcerer than a soldier. A black cape flowed behind him in the wind, giving him the appearance of a ghostlike phantom. Should the enemy mistake him for less than a warrior, they would find themselves at the mercy of a trained swordsman who could cut them to pieces without the aid of a single lick of magic. Magi were widely trained in all the arts, including the art of war.

Balthazar lowered his standard.

Across the battlefield, Molon watched the Greek soldiers load the catapults with large homemade looking projectiles. But they didn't look threatening. He decided to wait until they launched their first volley and then attack while they were loading for their second. This wasn't going to be a full-scale battle. Molon was merely engaging in a sortie to see how his enemy fought, figure out his battle patterns and maybe even strike some fear into them to demoralize their forces. When he was ready for all-out attack, he could minimize his own casualties by adjusting his strategy to his enemy's weaknesses. And he could see his enemy's first weakness was his reliance upon sorcerers. Such displays of magic might occasionally surprise or temporarily frighten an army, but in the end, battles were won with muscle, sweat, and blood, not magic tricks and spectacle.

When the catapults released, his suspicion was confirmed. They landed short of the army line in the desert plain, and exploded into clouds of grey dust upon impact with the ground.

They were testing the distance, charting it for accuracy with bags of chalk.

Fools, he thought, *Let them feel the terror of my Immortals*. The Immortals were the most renowned of the Persian warriors. They wore small-scaled armor beneath loose fitting fabric that was flexible and afforded the impression that their bodies were supernaturally protected. They fought in such tightly organized formation that if one was killed, another would take his place immediately, giving the appearance that they were in fact immortal.

Molon raised his sword and his brother Alexander blew his war horn.

The Immortals gave a cry of war that sent chills through the bones of the Greek warriors. Five hundred Median horsemen raced out in front of the lines and led the Immortals onto the field. They galloped through the chalky clouds on their way to pierce the defenses of their lesser Seleucid opponents.

But Molon now saw a line of archers behind the Greek forces raise flaming arrows into the air and release them. He watched with curiosity as the missiles arched through the sky like fiery lightning on their way toward his charging warriors.

Down below in the field, the cavalry was just breaking through the cloudy field, covered in the fine dust. The Immortals were in the midst of the dispersing cloud.

But then the arrows hit all around. They were not for the warriors. They were for the cloud. They lit the strange dust on fire. The grey smoke instantly became an inferno of orange flame that engulfed the unsuspecting horsemen and foot soldiers. The air itself was on fire. Those covered in the dust could not escape the burning. It was some kind of flammable substance that clung to their clothes.

Warriors screamed in searing pain. Horses fell to the ground. Men rolled around in the dirt, seeking to quench the flames. But they could not. Flesh melted from the bone in a frenzy of disoriented agony. Hundreds of them were burned alive in the firestorm.

Molon and his brother watched with terror.

"What sorcery is this?" muttered Alexander. "What black magic?"

Molon stared out onto the field of fire with dead eyes. "It is not black magic, brother. It is not magic at all. It is science—whose unknown nature is what ignorant man fears."

Xeneotas smiled as the black smoke of death rose from the desert plain. Molon's forces were demoralized.

"Magnificent, Balthazar."

The magus deferred, "I am but your servant."

They heard the horn of retreat and watched Molon's forces melt away.

Xeneotas quipped, "So much for superstitious omens of dread."

Xeneotas raised his sword and yelled to his warriors, "CHASE THEM INTO THE DESERT! KILL THEM IN THE ROCKS AND CRAGS!"

His herald blew the war horn and Xeneotas led his countercharge to chase them down.

Let Hades swallow them in chaos, thought Xeneotas.

The stench of burnt flesh stung his nostrils as they passed through the desert battle plain, filled with the scattered and blackened remains of bodies. The soldiers were charged with fury. Cries of victory bellowed from their throats.

Xeneotas saw the last remnants of Molon's forces disappear over the ridge. The Greek forces were almost upon them.

We have them now, thought Xeneotas. The king will finally acknowledge me. The world will know.

Xeneotas broke the ridge in the lead.

He pulled back on his reins at the sight before him. Five thousand armed Median and Persian warriors awaited him in silence below the steep incline.

He had just led his army into an ambush. It was the oldest tactic in the book, that worked against the oldest sin: pride.

His cavalry followed him down into the chaos.

It was too late to turn back now. He would have to fight. He would have to face the consequences of his own arrogance.

His horse was grounded by a flurry of arrows that just missed his own body. He rolled in the dirt and recovered his weapon, a *xyston*, a ten-foot long spear with iron blade-tips at each end. He was a master of the xyston. He wielded it with such expertise that he had slain ten men before they realized what was happening.

His infantry division crested the ridge to join them, but it was like diving into a swirling whirlpool of death.

Xeneotas was surrounded on every side by a circle of fighters. They pressed in. He swung with a mighty arc, thrust, and slashed, forward and reverse. He was a spinning wheel of fury. Within moments, twenty men were lying in a heap around him.

But there were hundreds behind them.

I deserve this death, he thought, as his weakening arms sought to stave off the unending swarm of attackers with hopeless dread.

But I will take as many of these criminals with me to the grave as I can.

CHAPTER 3

Xeneotas awoke in the dark. He could smell the dank musty air. He thought, *Am I in Hades?*

He groaned as a sharp pain pierced his ribs. His body ached all over. He tried to move, but he heard the clank of chains and felt their cold steel on his wrists. *Chains of Tartarus?* Tartarus was the lowest pit of Hades where the Titans were imprisoned. No. He was not *that* significant.

His eyes adjusted to the dark and he soon realized he was not dead. He was in a dungeon. Rancid water lay in still puddles. A rat scurried across the cell. Xeneotas tried to stand but fell back down to the ground with a dizzying pain from concussion.

Then his memory returned in fragments. Flashes of what had happened on the battlefield:

His horse crumbling to the ground by a flurry of arrows.

Crashing iron and bronze.

Splashing pools of blood.

His battalion massacred.

His arms weakening as he swung his xyston blade with fury.

Piles of bodies everywhere.

Sharp pain on the back of his head.

Blackout.

Flashes of a black wraith over him, cape flowing like a storm wind.

Small balls that exploded with fire from the hands of his savior.

Balthazar.

Rescued by the sorcery of his magus.

The sound of arriving guards and the unlocking of the cell door shook him out of his trance.

Four heavily armed guards dragged him down the hallway. Now he felt the full pain of his bruises and wounds.

He muttered, "My men. Where are my men?"

One of the guards, an ornery one, spit out with contempt, "All dead. Slaughtered like pigs by Molon."

Xeneotas felt as if a javelin had pierced his kidney. He had betrayed his king and failed his men. And now they were dead. Sacrificed for his pride. His pursuit of glory and respect of the crown had ruined him.

The other guard said, "Thank the gods the walls of the city kept Molon out. Hermias cleaned up your mess."

Xeneotas' eyes were blinded by the sunlight as they brought him through the palace courtyard.

Before he knew it, he was in the throne room of Antiochus the Great. He was back in Seleucia on the Tigris.

They dropped him to his knees at the foot of the throne, a large golden chair with lion cherubim cast on the sides. The king looked down upon him in silence.

Xeneotas looked up to see several generals and advisors standing beside the throne. Hermias, tall and imposing, stood closest. Xeneotas knew what his advice would be to the king. He just wasn't sure what form of death it would be.

At the outer circle stood Balthazar, stone-faced and silent. But a glance from his old friend assured him he was not alone.

Xeneotas *had* achieved a special audience with the king, but for dishonor instead of honor. He waited to hear his sentence. But the king remained silent for an unbearable count.

Then finally, Antiochus spoke. "Xeneotas, you have proven yourself a devoted and mighty leader in the past. That is why I gave you the command of Babylon."

Another moment of silence. The king's anger melted into genuine confusion. "What has bewitched you? Why did you think you could disobey my orders and live?"

Xeneotas would not speak. His teeth were clenched with bitterness.

Hermias drew his dagger and commanded, "Answer your king, soldier. Or die where you kneel."

Xeneotas spoke, "I did not seek to disobey. I sought for distinction."

The king said, "So you thought you would gain my attention with an heroic victory of great risk. Defiance of the odds."

The next was a genuine question from the king. "Glory to what purpose?"

The prisoner showed the king his hand. On it was a golden ring. A very familiar golden ring. The signet of the prince. *His* old signet ring. Confusion overcame Antiochus. Then fear.

He barked to this advisors, "Leave us, immediately. Except Hermias."

The advisors whisked out of the throne room. Hermias was his most trusted aide, and he would protect the king.

Antiochus glared at his captive. "Who are you?"

Xeneotas looked up at him.

Those dark thin eyes brought back a flood of memory to the king.

Xeneotas said, "My birth name is Antiochus the Younger."

This cannot not be, thought the king.

Xeneotas continued, "And that is what I want to be called in my death, because I will no longer hide my true identity." He pulled off the ring and held it out to the king.

Antiochus looked at it with dread. He would not touch it, as if it were cursed.

He said, "Where did you get that royal signet ring?"

Xeneotas stared into the king's soul. "From my mother."

Antiochus's kingdom crashed in on him. He felt dizzy. Short of breath.

He reached out and took the ring from his disgraced general's hand. He stared into it, and all the fading memories became clear again. He got down on his knees to look into the eyes of Xeneotas. A softness came over him. Compassion.

"My son," said the king.

Xeneotas could not look at him. "Your bastard son." He took a difficult breath. "Abandoned and forgotten."

Antiochus reached over and pulled Xeneotas' face up. Now he saw Thera's bold penetrating eyes looking back at him. He melted with grief. "This—is why you risked everything?"

Xeneotas said, "To face you. To claim my family name. To claim your…"

He could not finish the sentence. Antiochus thought, *To claim my throne?*

"To claim your love, my father."

Hermias was not so sentimental. He considered weeping, even familial weeping, to be a sign of weakness. "My lord, I beg your forgiveness in interrupting, but—the generals are already questioning your authority to stop this rebellion. They concur that your forces are overextended to the east. The Ptolemaic army is advancing upon Syria and Palestine to the west. And Roman naval forces are amassing in the Mediterranean. Weigh carefully the decision you are about to make."

Antiochus knew Hermias was right. And he dreaded what his general was going to say next.

"Xeneotas may be your son. But he is a bastard son, and he remains a criminal who defied the king's command. If you do not execute this *criminal*," he emphasized the word, "then I alone cannot stop their mutiny. Your kingdom is in dire jeopardy."

Bastards born of mistresses were of little significance for royal legacy, especially ones from unknown foreign kingdoms. It didn't matter that this was the son of Thera, his only true love. Kingdom and power transcended emotional attachments.

Antiochus stood over his son's broken posture.

"Return him to prison. He will be executed on the morrow."

Hermias bowed in obedience and pulled Xeneotas in his chains toward the exit.

The last look Xeneotas had of his father's face was a sad but hardened resolve. In his hand, the king gripped the signet ring, as if trying to crush it into dust.

Antiochus must be just. Xeneotas must die.

CHAPTER 4

The holy temple tower Etemenanki dominated the walled temple precinct of Babylon. Its name meant, "Temple of the foundation of heaven and earth." Temples were manmade holy mountains that connected the three-tiered universe of heaven above, the earth below, and the underworld beneath. This particular temple was a ziggurat, a large step-pyramid, one hundred fifty feet square at the bottom, that rose one hundred and fifty feet into the sky. The levels rose in successive stair-steps and the higher levels contained rooms and passageways.

Ziggurats were stairways to heaven where the gods would come down and meet with men. At the top was a sanctuary of Marduk, the king of the gods, where sacrifices were offered by the magi priests.

Balthazar held a sacrificial dagger to a goat laid upon a stone horned altar. The sanctuary was lit from several rays of the sun leaking through its small windows. One of those rays landed upon the goat's terrified eyes as Balthazar drew the blade across its throat.

The goat gurgled and kicked but Balthazar held it firm until it relaxed in his arms. Its life bled out of it onto the altar and down the blood channels.

Two other magi stood in prayer beside Balthazar. These were Melchior, the eldest of the three, and Gaspar, pudgy with bright eyes.

They prayed to the image of Marduk, a large stone statue of the king of the gods carved out of hard black obsidian stone. *The Enuma Elish*, the Babylonian epic poem of creation, told the story of how Tiamat, the sea dragon of chaos, threatened to destroy the other gods of the pantheon. None could stop her, until Marduk the god of vegetation and storm accepted the challenge. But he imposed one condition. If he returned victorious, the rest of the pantheon would submit to him as king. The gods accepted his terms and he went out to battle.

Tiamat called up many powerful monsters to fight Marduk, but he won the war with his battle net, mace and bow, crushing the skull of the sea dragon. He then tore Tiamat's body in half to create the heavens and the earth. He set all the stars in their place, the astral gods, to rule according to his sovereign will. And that was how Marduk became the king of the gods as well as the patron deity of the city of Babylon.

That divine statue looked down upon the magi priests. Marduk was adorned in his battle skirt with perfectly coifed square beard, horned headdress of deity, and carrying his battle net and mace.

The purpose of cult images was not to be worshipped as gods. Rather, the devotees believed they were representations of the god's presence that operated as windows of access to the deity. They performed ceremonies to "call down the breath" of the god into the image, so as to establish a connection for communication.

Balthazar raised his hands toward the black image and said, "Mighty Marduk, accept this sacrifice on behalf of General Xeneotas. Have mercy upon him. Grant him a quick death."

Gaspar lit several censors of incense whose smoky haze began to fill the room.

Suddenly, everyone was aware of an odor. But it was not the incense. It was a distinctly repugnant odor. One they were all familiar with.

Melchior, the thinner magus, gave a dirty look to the squat Gaspar, who glanced guiltily back at him. Gaspar whispered, "I am sorry. You should not have used those herbs in the meal. They do not agree with me."

Melchior hissed, "Brother, can you not hold it in during sacred devotions?"

Gaspar whispered back, "Brother, you know onions do not sit well with my digestion."

Melchior rolled his eyes.

"Quiet, you two," whispered Balthazar. "And thank the gods for the overbearing scent of the incense." His remarks were punctuated with a wily upturn of his lips.

He returned to his prayers.

They all became lightheaded as the smell of the incense now took over their olfactory senses. The room filled with a haze of trance-like ecstasy.

Melchior welcomed the vision-inducing incense as a diversion to his depressing life. A chance to forget the world around him, a world of disappointment. He had studied the philosophy of sages to discover their secret wisdom, but all it had produced in him was despair. For this was a world of power, not ideas. Men of power and action ruled and shaped the world to their whims. Men of ideas could only hope to influence men of power, as Aristotle did Alexander, but they could not be the instrument of change.

Melchior's only hope for such influence was to become the next high priest, a position that had been slated for the son of the high priest, Balthazar. After Balthazar turned it down, the position was now an open consideration for other magi in the order. Melchior wanted it, but knew his standing was not favorable among the other magi. He had been too pushy with his intellectual agenda and some of the order resented him for it. They would most likely never vote him high priest of the magi. So Melchior let the incense carry him away in escape from his hopeless desires.

Balthazar breathed in the fumes deeply. As a devoted magus priest, he embraced whatever helped to release himself from the earth and connect with the heavenly realm. He had a deeply Platonic view of reality. This world and all its physicality and power was a mere shadow of the true world of the ideal forms. The pursuit of the perfect, unchangeable eternal truth was what drove him, not the ever-changing vicissitudes of a world drunk on worldly power. He felt the only way he could achieve his spiritual quest was to renounce this world and its physical imperfections. It was why he had already rejected the opportunity to become the next high priest of the magi. Because his own father was in that position and had become so thoroughly corrupted by the power that Balthazar had turned it down when it was offered him upon his father's recent death. Balthazar sought virtue, not power.

Gaspar considered the incense a necessary annoyance that obscured his ability to think clearly, something he preferred not to experience. He had experimented with many substances so he knew what physical results they created in the worshippers. In fact, his experimental knowledge was a kind of curse to him, because it gave him doubts about spiritual realities. His studies of the sciences of astrology, sorcery, and military technologies, made him a man of the physical world. And that world operated with a consistency and uniformity that lent itself more to the nature of laws than gods. Such profane thoughts were not acceptable in this world, so he aspired to the office of high priest, where he thought he might gain enough respect to institute reforms without being tried for apostasy. So when Balthazar had rejected the position, Gaspar placed his hopes upon his achievements of invention as granting him an advantage for the post. For instance, he had created the fire balls of death used in the battle against Molon. Unfortunately, though the sorcery worked quite well, Xeneotas had lost that battle, which significantly reduced the odds of gaining the necessary notoriety for Gaspar.

The three magi floated within their own worlds of thought as they prayed kneeling in the haze with holy obeisance toward Marduk.

Balthazar thought he heard a scraping sound. He opened his eyes.

He blinked several times to make sure he was seeing clearly.

The obsidian image was surrounded by the scented fog. But through the hazy blur, he could swear he saw a figure next to the stone image. It looked exactly like the image. But it looked alive.

Was this the hallucinatory effect of the incense?

The sound of Gaspar and Melchior gasping told Balthazar that they too saw this phantasm. Could it be a mass delusion? Were they all drugged by their own sorcery?

The figure moved toward them, parting the mist.

They all took a step back in fear.

Gaspar began to sweat. Melchior's mouth went dry.

The great figure was eight feet tall. He strode to the altar and put his hands on the dead goat, while watching the three magi.

He was an awesome being. Frightening to behold. His eyes were lapis lazuli blue, with reptilian thin slivers of pupils. His skin had a sparkling quality like that of burnished bronze that would glitter in the rays of light that leaked in. Balthazar thought, *A Shining One.* When he spoke, his voice seemed to penetrate into their minds exposing their pathetic existence as finite creatures of flesh.

Marduk was calm but firm. "I will protect Xeneotas. You must prepare for defense. A secret enemy approaches."

Balthazar thought, A secret enemy approaches? What does that mean? What kind of enemy? From where? From which corner of the earth? Has Molon breached our walls?

Suddenly, the sound of a horned alert bellowed throughout the temple.

Melchior shouted, "The temple is under attack!"

Balthazar drew his sword and shouted as he ran for the door, "The relics! We must protect the relics!"

He opened the door and let the magi brothers leave first. He looked back to see Marduk at the altar, sucking the blood out of the dead goat's body.

They had just survived an encounter with the king of the gods.

CHAPTER 5

The three magi, Balthazar, Melchior and Gaspar, sprinted through the dark hallways below the temple altar.

They rounded a corner and slid to a stop behind a contingent of fifteen Seleucid temple guards. Before them were five enemy warriors. Strange foreigners that they had never seen before. They wore small leather platelets draped over them like a long cloak with flowing red robes beneath them. Their swords looked oversized and had open slits in them. They had no helmets. All of them had long black hair that was wrapped up into a bun on the top of their heads. But their eyes were the strangest of all. They were almond-like thin and they lacked eyelids.

Are these monsters of Tiamat? thought Balthazar. Where did they come from? What do they want?

The magi drew their swords. They saw their goal, a door to the archives, that was between them and the intruders.

Melchior said to their guards, "You must push forward. We need to get to the archives!"

The leader of the guard grunted acknowledgment and they moved forward to engage the enemy.

Gaspar added, "We must save the relics."

"We know, Gaspar," said Melchior. "No need to repeat the obvious."

That was when they noticed the leader of the foreign warriors. He stepped forward in such a way that it appeared the other four were merely his backup. He was not a large or burly warrior, but compact, confident and calculated. His strange eyes were fearless, he did not wear armor, but exotic robes. And he carried an eight-foot pole with a sword sized blade at the end of it. The magi had never seen anything like it. Ornate, ceremonial looking. Gaspar thought to himself, *Why didn't I think of inventing a weapon like that? It's brilliant.*

The temple guards attacked.

The single warrior engaged the fifteen Seleucids with his "glaive" pole blade. His moves were more like dance than like battle. Balthazar became so entranced by the beauty of his warrior ballet he forgot his duty.

"Balthazar!" yelled Melchior. "The relics!"

Gaspar and Melchior had drawn their weapons and pushed Balthazar toward the doorway.

The foreign warrior had taken down five of the Seleucids in moments.

Balthazar unlocked the door.

Two more were down. The foreigner jumped and dodged the enemy swords like he was light as a feather. A dancing feather—of death.

They could see he would be to the door in seconds.

Balthazar turned to let the two others in, but Melchior and Gaspar stayed outside and pushed the door shut. Balthazar stumbled backward.

"No!" he screamed and tried to open the door.

Behind it, he heard Melchior yell, "Save the relics!"

Balthazar yelled again, "Melchior!" but he bolted the door behind him, because they had all taken vows to protect the relics above their lives.

Gaspar shouted to Melchior, "I thought you said not to repeat the obvious!"

Melchior ignored it and stepped in front of Gaspar, facing the enemy. "Little brother, I know you want to be the next high priest! Remember my death as making it possible!"

Gaspar nudged him aside. "Not so fast, older brother. You want to be high priest too! You are not going to get the glory this time!"

They lunged forward together to meet their approaching adversary.

Inside the archives room, Balthazar could hear the blades clanging outside. He knew they would not last. His magi brothers were not skilled fighters. And the foreign warrior had preternatural skills. But he prayed they would hold him off just long enough for Balthazar to get the holy relics to safety.

He turned to the library of shelves full of scrolls and tablets. In the center of the wall at the far side was a holy shrine lit by torchlight. He approached it cautiously.

When he stood before it, he glanced up at a Babylonian brick painting that operated as a backdrop to the shrine. Fired blue brick with scenes of Babylonian past. A victory in the western land of Judea. An exile of a captive foreign peoples. Brought to slavery in the great city during the reign of Nebuchadnezzar II. And one of the treasures, a large golden candelabra from the enemy's temple. The story of their captive booty.

He reached down and opened ornately carved wooden doors and pulled out two sacred artifacts. One, a small golden jar, covered, and engraved with a foreign tongue, the other, a crude three foot wooden staff.

These holy relics. Deceptive in their humility. Infused with the magical power of a foreign god. Captured from the very people from whom Balthazar's own order of magi had long ago learned secrets of the universe. The Hebrews.

When the Hebrew captives returned to their land after seventy years of exile in Babylon, the order of magi retained these relics. They had been removed from a golden box called "the ark of the covenant." which had been hidden by one of their prophets and never confiscated by the Babylonians. But the magi, under the tutelage of the Hebrew prophet named Daniel, were sworn to guard these retrieved relics with their lives. And so they had through the centuries. It was the only reason Balthazar left his comrades to fight. They all were devoted to a higher cause than their lives.

Balthazar turned a hidden latch and the shrine opened to reveal a secret passageway in the walls.

But before he could make his way, he noticed the sounds of battle had ceased outside the door. No one was trying to break into the archives. Were they gone? Were his fellow magi dead?

He should not have hesitated. But he loved his priestly companions. They were annoying at times, and hardheaded. Endlessly competitive. But he loved them as brothers. They were his spiritual family.

Balthazar held his ear against the door listening for the slightest hint of sound, the barest possibility of subterfuge. He could hear nothing but his own heavy breathing. He wanted to open the door to find out. If he was wrong, he could end up dead.

But he had to find out. He drew his sword, ready to kill. He unbarred the door, and slowly peeked through the crack of an opening with the sound of a creaking hinge.

He saw the bodies on the floor, strewn all about. All the Seleucid temple guards were dead. One of the foreign mercenaries laid near the door, though this one had no battle armor, but wore a white robe with black sash and trimming, now stained with the blood of battle. The robe and sash had strange symbols on them, he had never seen before.

No wait. He *had* seen them somewhere before. Where was it?

His curiosity got the better of him. He opened the creaking door and presented his arms in defense. There were no warriors in hiding. No one to jump at him with surprise.

But why? Surely, they had seen him enter the room.

And where were Melchior and Gaspar?

One of the temple guards moaned. Balthazar ran to his side. He was barely alive, but would not be for long. Balthazar bent down and cradled the poor soul's head.

"What happened?"

The guard struggled to get out his last words. "Th-they took them. Melchior and Gaspar. Kidnapped."

And then the guard relaxed in the arms of death like a human sacrifice for the demands of a foreign god.

Kidnapped? Why? The king must be alerted to this intrusion. It may be a scouting mission for a foreign invasion, thought Balthazar. But first, I have something more important to do.

Balthazar heard a soft moan from the foreigner. He was still alive.

CHAPTER 6

Xeneotas sat in chains in the dreary dungeon cell. He was ragged, beaten, hopeless. But for the first time in his life, he felt free. He had faced his father the king, revealed his secret, and claimed his ancestry. Now, he was going to die.

The sound of an arriving visitor and the clinking of the keys in the lock aroused him. At the dungeon door, a cloaked and hooded figure was escorted by guards. The executioner.

He walked into the cell like a wraith of death, but the guards stayed behind. What was this?

The figure took off his hood. Xeneotas whispered with a gasp, "Balthazar."

The magus knelt down and described to Xeneotas everything that had just happened at the temple. The alien scouts, the kidnapping of the magi, the possibility of foreign invasion.

Balthazar drew out a metallic pick. He inserted it into Xeneotas' shackles and they softly clicked open.

"I am here to help you escape," whispered the magus. "I want you to help me rescue my magi brothers."

Xeneotas looked at him, "You are mad."

Balthazar rejoined, "You are the only one I trust. Is our lifelong friendship of no value to you?"

"That is why I refuse," complained Xeneotas. "I will not let you join me in my death sentence."

"There is something else I did not tell you," said Balthazar. "Before the attack, I had a vision of Marduk and he told me he would protect you."

Xeneotas gave him a scolding look.

Balthazar said, "*That* is why I did not tell you."

"And which deity would protect you, my friend?"

"I care nothing for my fate in this world," said Balthazar. He paused to consider, then said, "I have told you before, but you refuse to believe. The stars predict that one day an emperor will come down from heaven and will rule the world with justice."

Xeneotas turned sad in his stare. "Balthazar, you run from power to your gods and prophecies. Only human power can bring justice."

Balthazar disagreed, "Human power leads to tyranny and madness if it is not under the power of heaven."

Xeneotas could only hang his head as he whispered. "I will not let you rescue me." He snapped his shackles back together. "I only offer my heartfelt goodbye to a loyal magus and friend."

Balthazar remained silent, refusing to let him win. But finally, he knew he could not save a man who would not be saved.

"My captain, my friend."

They sat in silence knowing that tomorrow Xeneotas would die.

CHAPTER 7

A single bright beam of sunlight spilled in through the slit of a window in the dungeon cell. It moved slowly across the wall with the rising of the morning sun.

It landed on the closed eye of Xeneotas, who awakened with a blink and stared into the brightness. It was like a ray of fire burning away the impurities of a soul.

Awaken to your death, O man.

Xeneotas sat forward as if prompted by unseen knowledge. He then heard the sound of guards down the hall approaching his cell. The clink of the key in the lock sounded louder than it ever had. The hinge creakier. The footsteps of his executioners more intense and weightier as they hit the floor, gravel crunching beneath their feet. Now that he was going to his death, his senses had come alive to amplify every last moment with clarity.

There was only one executioner. A big, bad, ugly Mycenaean. Xeneotas thought with more clarity and rapidity than ever before. Did they craft these men to fit the part? Did they feed them diseased meat to grow their height and rot their teeth? Did they deliberately carve scars into their faces and arms to make them look more like the harbingers of death that they were?

He smiled with amusement.

The executioner tossed a black hood at Xeneotas. He willingly put it over his own head. It would not mask the sounds that he could still hear with magnification around him.

The brute led his prisoner out of the cell for his final journey.

Though the hood blocked his sight, the bound and hooded prisoner could see some shadowy forms in the sunlight through the fabric. He could hear the crowd of people filling the square with shouts of outrage and anger. He could swear he heard each individual shout.

"Traitor!"

"You deserve death!"

"Xeneotas, say hello to Pluto!" The god of the underworld.

He felt the sting of rotten food hitting him in the body and in the head. One piece was so putrid, the stench soaked through the fabric and made him gag.

The guards pulled him along through the gauntlet of abuse to a platform. He tripped on the first stair and fell to his knees. The guards caught him, but not before he felt a searing pain shoot through his knee. He grunted. The humiliation of the walk was worse for him than the punishment at the end of it. It was one thing to execute a man, but to reduce him to a stumbling buffoon was more degrading.

The executioner's axe maintained his dignity because it was an exalted ritual act that reinforced the sacred notion of the prisoner's human worth. Only a man in the image of a god had the divine conscience to know right and wrong. Mere animals are not punished because they have no such dignity. They may be slaughtered, but they are not punished.

But all that dignity was stripped from him by the time he reached the block. He was shoved to his knees. More stinging pain. He could hear the breathing of his captors as they pushed his hooded head upon the block. His breathing became shallow and quickened. He felt his entire body fill with a surge of tingling energy. The crowds continued their verbal abuse.

A satrap governor quieted them down and announced, "People of the kingdom of Seleucia, hear now the crime of this condemned man, General Xeneotas of Babylon, who disobeyed a direct order of the king, and as a result led his force of four thousand men to their deaths at the hands of the rebel general, Molon!"

Boos and hisses arose to drown out the satrap. When they died down, he continued. "For his crimes against the royal monarch's authority and power and glory, Xeneotas of Babylon now receives his punishment, the removal of his head from his body. May the gods have mercy on his soul!"

More boos and shouts of "Rot in Hades!"

The executioner stood over him. The condemned criminal's head rested on the block but his body was shuddering.

Another guard pulled off the hood and stepped away.

He could not see the generals lined up behind him, eagerly awaiting justice. He could not see the crowd below him. He only saw the executioner raise the axe above his head. Heard the sound of his grunt.

And the blade came down with swift and sure accuracy.

The crowd cheered with vengeance and bloodlust.

CHAPTER 8

The black hood was pulled from the head of Xeneotas. He coughed and squinted as his eyes adjusted to the bright light of day. Judging by the sounds and pathway, he had guessed correctly where he was: the king's war room. The king and Balthazar stood before him with a strange looking foreigner. He had been here many a time in consultation for battle strategy. But why? Why had he not been executed? Was this merely a ruse?

Xeneotas asked humbly, "My king?"

Antiochus said, "I have executed a man in your place. Another criminal who looked like you."

It didn't register immediately to Xeneotas.

"My generals think you are dead and I am safe from their mutiny. For now."

Xeneotas now understood what had happened. The king had mercy upon him. His father could not escape the guilty haunt of his beloved, and the fruit of their union.

"However," said the king, "the rebellion continues with Molon's forces amassing. He is marching upon this capital. He is calling himself king."

Xeneotas interrupted, "Molon must be crushed. Like the revolt of the Parthians and Bactrians years ago."

The king began to pace. "Ah, yes, and that is where we find ourselves again. As with my father, so my power has been spread too thin over too vast of territory."

Xeneotas glanced at Balthazar. It was confirmation of his own counsel to the king.

"My generals tell me to stop wasting forces on distant insignificant lands like Judea." Xeneotas knew Balthazar had favor for the Hebrews because of his order's great respect for their ancient magus Daniel.

The king sighed. "The collapse of my kingdom is imminent." Xeneotas could not believe he was hearing this admission. Was the king giving up?

"And that is where you come in, Xeneotas." The king gestured to Balthazar to speak.

Xeneotas looked to the magus, but saw the foreigner next to him. He suddenly realized just how familiar the man looked. His skin was not white or black, but olive. He wore a gleaming embroidered robe with ornate flower patterns and serpentine images. The fabric was unique, soft and flowing. The foreigner's eyes were different, thin, mysterious. Such peculiarities would ordinarily be attributed to barbarians, but this was no barbarian. He reminded Xeneotas of his mother.

Balthazar said, "This is Chang Shen. He comes from a distant land called *Tianxia*. It means 'all under heaven.' They believe themselves the center of all the earth."

The king gave an amused smirk to himself. Everyone knew Greece was the center of the earth.

Balthazar continued, "He was wounded and left for dead by the foreign strike force that kidnapped some of our magi. I found him."

Xeneotas knew where this was going. Balthazar had already told him of this incident. But this captive did not look like a warrior.

As if answering his thoughts, Balthazar said, "Chang is a scholar for his people. Much like a magus. But he would not tell us why they kidnapped our magi."

"How well do you understand his language?"

"Barely. I recognized it from the ancient archives I studied in our library. They were inscribed on oracle bones. Generations ago, King Cyrus over Babylonia had contact with these people from the far eastern ends of the earth."

Xeneotas hid his surprise. Could these be his mother's people? He asked, "Why were they hidden? Why have we never heard of 'Tianxia?'"

Xeneotas' mother had died when he was young. She had told him only mysterious fables and fairy tales. She had not mentioned Tianxia.

The king joined in, "Because Cyrus decided it was a land he could not conquer." It was common for potentates to hide their failures from written records.

Xeneotas didn't believe it. "The mighty Cyrus? Unable to conquer? Why not?"

Balthazar looked at the king for approval. Antiochus nodded.

He said, "Because it was a land of dragons."

Xeneotas said nothing. He narrowed his eyes with incredulity. The king is interested in fairy tales? The kind of tales Xeneotas heard as a child?

Antiochus said, "I spared you, Xeneotas, for this reason. I have a mission for you that will redeem you, and my kingship. I want you to go to Tianxia and bring me back a dragon."

Xeneotas' incredulity became amusement.

"I will secure my reign with its power, and you will resurrect yourself as a hero—and inherit my kingdom."

Xeneotas' eyes went wide. But then his countenance dropped. "My lord, dragons are but myths of power created to inspire fear of the ruler in the ruled."

"Then go and prove me wrong." He smiled. "You are dead anyway."

Xeneotas looked to Balthazar for support. He received none.

He looked back to the king. "If there were such a creature with such power, how could I possibly capture it?"

"That is why Balthazar is going with you. He will use his magic."

Balthazar gave no response. Not even a shrug of resignation. Xeneotas did not know if everyone around him was going mad, or just himself. He decided to play along. Use the madness against itself.

"My lord, such monsters cannot be tamed to your will. They are agents of chaos."

"I will unleash the chaos upon my enemies."

The king *was* mad.

"You may unleash it upon yourself."

"Just get me the dragon, Xeneotas. I will deal with the rest. I am the king."

He paused. Then added, "And you will be my son—if you succeed. Xeneotas of Seleucia."

The foreigner understood none of their words.

Xeneotas thought, *Am I escaping death only to disappear into oblivion? But then again, if these foreigners come from the land of my mother…*

He said, "Xeneotas is dead. He was executed. My name is Antiochus the Younger. And I will go to the ends of the earth in search of your dragon."

The king grinned victoriously. He said, "I am curious as well to learn about this foreign land called Tianxia. I expect a full report."

I am sure you do, thought the Younger. He bowed. After all these years of desiring to find his home with the king of this land, he thought it ironic that he might now find that home on the other side of the world.

49

CHAPTER 9

Xeneotas, now known as Antiochus the Younger, stood in his ship's quarters with Balthazar and Chang on their way down the Euphrates toward the gulf of the Southern Sea. The ride was smooth as they had not yet reached the gulf in their trireme, a long thin warship hosting a company of over forty warriors. The trireme got its name for its three tiers of oars rowed by a crew of one hundred seventy oarsmen that gave them maneuverability in battle. It was not a comfortable vessel for long voyages, but it was swift and efficient.

Xeneotas pointed at the map laid out on his table. It contained the entire Seleucid empire from Greece in the west, to the Levant, Mesopotamia and all the way to Bactria and Parthia in the east.

"The trip to Tianxia will take months. We will travel from the Southern Sea, into the Arabian Sea, where we will make several stops at ports of the Mauryan Empire on our way east. But beyond this point, we sail the unknown."

He pointed beyond the drawn image of the East Indian continent to an unfinished blank space. Their mapmakers had no reliable sources to reconstruct the mysterious eastern ends of the earth.

Chang watched Antiochus' gestures closely. He could not understand his words, but he could understand the visual map. He reached into a bag he carried with him and pulled out a small bottle and paintbrush.

As he removed the top and dipped the brush into the bottle, Antiochus asked Balthazar, "Where did he get those instruments?"

"He asked me for them before we left."

The Eastern man placed his ink-dipped brush to the map. Antiochus reached out to stop him reflexively.

"Let him," said Balthazar.

Antiochus withdrew and Chang began to paint in the blank area of the map. He filled in the land mass with a line that illustrated his own knowledge of the area. He drew some islands they would have to pass through to get to Tianxia. Then up in the far eastern corner, he brushed in a little bay with a river going inland. He drew a strange looking symbol at the mouth of the river. His hand moved with a graceful speed. Lines and swashes created a pictogram that Antiochus thought was both mysterious and beautiful. It was their written language.

Chang said, "Langya."

Balthazar repeated, "Langya," and Chang smiled with a nod.

"It must be the port city to enter their kingdom."

Chang drew a dotted course from where their ship was currently on the map all the way to Langya. He looked up at them with a smile and a bowed head.

Antiochus said, "This foreigner smiles and bows with a frequency quite annoying."

"It is their custom," said Balthazar. "We will have some time to learn their ways in preparation for our diplomacy."

Antiochus smirked. "If you call hostage exchange 'diplomacy.'"

He smiled at Chang and added, "Yes, my dear foreigner. You will be our bargaining shekel to retrieve our magi. At least, that is the pretense for our ulterior motive."

Chang smiled and bowed his head innocently in return.

"Be careful," said Balthazar. "He may understand more than we know."

Balthazar pointed at the strange symbol and looked at Chang. "The place to begin learning a nation's custom is to learn their language."

He smiled at Chang, pointed to his own lips, then to Chang's lips, and then back to the symbol. Chang smiled and bowed.

Antiochus said, "You two wise men will get along splendidly, I see. I can only imagine your endless chatter about stars, gods, and divination once you learn his language."

Balthazar said, "Oh, you will be learning it as well, general."

Antiochus' smile drooped with displeasure.

• • • • •

Balthazar and Chang worked tirelessly for days to establish a basic means of understanding each other's language. After a couple weeks, Antiochus finally joined them for the first time in Balthazar's quarters on the ship. He stood back in surprise. "What in Hades?"

He hadn't seen them pack the boat before he was commissioned. Balthazar's entire quarters was packed tight with boxes from floor to ceiling, leaving little room for a bed and a small table. Some of the boxes had been opened to reveal a shipload of scrolls and tablets as well as some special devices of magi science.

Balthazar said, "If I am supposed to help you catch a dragon, General, I am going to need all my resources."

Antiochus said, "If the ship needs to lose ballast, I am afraid we will have to start here."

Balthazar looked at the smiling Chang and said, "My dear Chang, we men of education must impress upon this man of action the importance of knowledge and science, else he find himself afloat on a sea without a compass to guide him." Chang grinned in response.

Antiochus gave Balthazar a scorned look. "Show me what you've learned, man of education."

They sat down at the table, with the boxes towering over them. Balthazar pulled some parchment out with the oriental language written all over it.

"I had spent time with the oracle bones in our archives, so I was already familiar with some of the patterns of their communication."

He pointed at the writing on the parchment. "Their words are like pictures. And stories. They combine some phonetics with pictograms and ideograms. Phonetics are, of course, audible sounds. Pictograms are somewhat pictorial, and ideograms are complex combinations of pictograms for more abstract ideas."

"Balthazar, I do not want an academic discourse. I need to learn the basics."

"Sorry," said Balthazar. "They write from the top to the bottom, instead of left to right as we do." That seemed so unnatural to Antiochus. He wondered if these people did everything upside down or backwards.

"Boat"

Balthazar pointed to one pictogram. "To the point. This is the word for 'boat.'"

The image was not recognizable to Antiochus, so Balthazar gestured to the various components. "This element means 'vessel,' and this means 'eight mouths,' or people on that vessel.

"Why eight people?" asked Antiochus.

"They believe in a primeval flood. A great deluge that drowned all living things save a family of eight. Their language embodies their cultural stories and myths."

Antiochus knew that was similar to their own Greek myth of Deucalion, the son of Prometheus, whose life was spared along with his wife, Pyrrha, from a devastating flood. But they were only two. Who were the other six these foreigners were including in their story?

Balthazar showed him another word on the parchment. "This is their word for emperor, which is the same as our king." The brush strokes were fluid looking, but still did not make sense to Antiochus.

Balthazar continued, "The emperor of Tianxia is named Ch'in Shih Huang Di."

Antiochus tried to reproduce the name as Chang watched him. "Chin Shuh H-wong Dee." Chang smiled and nodded. He said "Yes, yes," in Greek and then followed with gibberish in his own language.

Balthazar said, "Ch'in is the family dynasty name. Like Seleucid for our king. 'Huang Di' was the name of the originator of their civilization."

Antiochus said, "Tell me more of this emperor and his 'Ch'inese' people."

Balthazar said, "From what I gather, the people of Tianxia have lived under battling warlords for centuries. Huang Di is the first emperor to unite all under heaven, according to Chang."

"*All* under heaven? He is evidently unaware of the Seleucid kingdom. So this emperor has an inflated view of himself."

"As does our king."

Antiochus gave him a scolding look.

Balthazar added some crude brush strokes to the word "emperor."

"This is the addition of the concept 'under heaven.' It is their word for a single god, 'Shang Di,' the Emperor of Heaven."

"Shang Di"

The magus turned more serious. "Antiochus, my order of magi have a star prophecy that the King of Heaven will yet come with a star in the east. He will unite all nations under heaven. That is strikingly similar with this Ch'inese belief. It seems all nations seek the same hope."

Antiochus was more skeptical. "It seems all rulers seek the same godlike power."

"There is more," said Balthazar. "Look here." He pulled out another parchment with other Ch'inese words on it. "This is the word for 'tempter.'"

"Tempter"

He carefully caressed each brush stroke as he explained the meaning. "This is the ideogram for 'devil,' and 'secret man.'

"Devil"

This glyph originally meant 'serpent." This square is a garden. These are two trees, and this is a covering. The word for 'tempter' is the story of the devil as a serpent in a garden with two trees. Under the cover of one tree, the serpent whispers secrets with the words of a man. It is a story of primeval temptation."

"What do I care for such myths?" said Antiochus.

"Because by learning a culture's myths, you understand how they think."

Antiochus continued to listen. He respected Balthazar. Though they were divided over such things as religion and politics, he had proven to be of wise counsel to Antiochus over the years. He knew he should listen even if he was skeptical. And he did want to understand these Ch'inese people. So he had better learn.

Balthazar was like a little boy with exciting new toys. "See this? This is the word for 'tower.'"

"Tower"

Again, Antiochus saw all the markings as gibberish. But he watched as the magus pointed out each element of the word. "This means 'mankind,' and this means 'one.' This is 'mouth' or 'speech,' and this is 'united' or 'joined together.' While this last piece of the pictogram represents 'undertaking' and 'clay brick.' So the word for 'tower' is a story that Chang says took place after the Flood. It tells of all mankind being of one language. They join together to undertake the building of a clay brick tower."

Antiochus had trouble following the point of it. He had studied military history and strategy, not so much the myths of the people. Although he did know the epic of Gilgamesh well, because Gilgamesh was a mighty giant warrior king of Uruk just after the Great Flood, and the most renowned of legendary heroes in Mesopotamia. He was known as "wild bull on the rampage," "one third mortal and two thirds divine." His relationship with the "wild born" Enkidu of the Steppe reminded Antiochus of his own relationship with Balthazar. Like the magi, Enkidu was more primal, less sophisticated than his king companion. But they became a heroic team that slew Humbaba the Terrible, a giant who ruled the Great Cedar Forest, and the Bull of Heaven, a fearsome behemoth that terrorized Uruk.

Antiochus mused over this similarity with he and Balthazar going to capture a dragon. Would they become a legend as well? Would they be able to face a fire breathing reptilian armored monster and bring him back with glory? But of course, there are no dragons, only the imaginations of earth-bound men who long for transcendent purpose and dignity through their legends and myths.

Balthazar's words broke Antiochus out of his day dreaming. "The Ch'inese story of the Tower is exactly like our own Sumerian tale of Enmerker and the Lord of Aratta. Enmerker sought to build a ziggurat of fired bricks on the plain of Shinar. But the god Enki came and confused the languages of the people, and they spread out upon the face of the earth. But that is not the only comparison."

Antiochus said, "What do you mean?"

"Well, the Hebrews, when they were exiled in Babylon, they too told of ancient days where the tongues of nations were confused and spread out on the land. The tower was our own Etemenanki in Babylon. They called it 'Babel.'"

"Confusion"

Antiochus was catching on. "So, these Ch'inese originally come from the dispersal of nations at Babylon?"

Balthazar nodded. "That is why they have similar stories with our own. Chang's mercenaries were returning to the tower of their origin for some reason."

"But why kidnap magi priests?"

"That, our friendly smiling Chang still refuses to divulge. We need more time to learn his language."

Antiochus said, "These written characters are too complex for the time I have. Let us focus on the spoken word."

"I am but your servant," said Balthazar.

That night, Antiochus could not sleep. It was not the rocking of the waves that kept him awake, but the restlessness of his thoughts. Could this distant mysterious land hold the answers to his own longing? He had been so young when his mother died. She had told him the secret of his father and how he was a child of the king. But she had never told him of her own history. She had deliberately hid it from him. A person's ancestry determined so much in this world. Because of her own lowly status, he could only imagine that she didn't want him to be at a disadvantage. She had wanted him to rise to power within this world that he knew by embracing it as his own. And that could not be achieved if he was torn in his soul between two identities, a mongrel rejected by two worlds.

But he remembered the stories. They haunted his dreams. She would put him to bed with wondrous tales of a magical land of fantasy. A world of one hundred states and one hundred schools of thought. Wise sages with strange foreign names and curious religious beliefs. The dragons in the stories had convinced him they were the product of a creative imagination, but now he was not so sure what was real and what was imagined.

He had entered military school through the royal mandate, and had risen through the ranks because of his hungry and tireless pursuit of victory to prove himself. But he never saw his mother again. She died shortly after he entered the school and his humble origins died with her.

He had been raised a Seleucid Greek, but because of his secret identity, he had always felt like a man without a country.

He felt so drawn to this mysterious new land of its own secrets. But would it be his redemption or his destruction?

CHAPTER 10

Days turned into weeks, and weeks into months for their ocean journey into the unknown east. They had stopped at several ports for supplies, but they were now relying upon Chang's cartography and navigation as they made their way through a chain of islands into the unexplored sea.

Balthazar had set his mind to understanding the language of Tianxia and was able to speak with a moderate level of understanding. Antiochus had the responsibility of the ship, so he was only able to gain enough knowledge of key words for communicating, more like a child. He still needed translation for complex conversation.

Chang, for his part, was as eager as his fellow scholar magus in his own efforts at learning the Greek language. Balthazar felt like he had found a kindred spirit, someone who understood him and experienced the world from an intellectually curious perspective.

However, there were significant differences between the Greek and Ch'inese cultures.

Balthazar considered Greek tradition to be individualistic and quite direct with their communication. Their heritage of philosophers gave them a pride in clarity and precision of language. The Ch'inese on the other hand were more collectivist in culture and indirect with their communication. Chang seemed overly polite to him, and was more opaque with his emotions. It was as if they sought to never stand out from the community. Balthazar would laugh heartily at a joke or mistake during their learning, while Chang would only smile and look downward.

But over the weeks, Balthazar saw a change in his scholarly companion. Chang had as much curiosity about Mesopotamia and the Seleucids as Balthazar had about Tianxia and the Ch'inese. He asked as many questions about Aristotle as Balthazar asked about Confucius, their most influential Ch'inese philosopher.

Antiochus did not tell either of them that he recognized the name Confucius from his mother's stories. So it wasn't all fantasy, after all.

Balthazar learned that Confucius taught much practical wisdom and common sense that sounded quite similar to Aristotle's Nichomachean ethics. Ch'inese culture was hierarchal and consisted of four basic "occupations" or classes in descending order: scholars, farmers, artisans and merchants. As one of the members in the emperor's Academy of Scholars, Chang had borne the experience of privilege.

The Central Kingdom of Tianxia had a long legacy of warring feudal states, that were only recently unified under the victorious conquering emperor. But one of the reforms the emperor instituted was the replacement of Confucianism with Legalism, a martial philosophy that stressed the law of the ruler as a monopoly over the feudal magnates of each people. Such unified standards and law broke down the power that regional cultures had on the people. Everyone was treated the same "under heaven," by the same standard, and that standard was the emperor's own. This application was achieved through three central concepts: power, method, and law.

Chang on the other hand became fascinated with the Hellenism of the west. The Greek gymnasiums and baths, their obsession with sport, and the perfection of the body. He was most amazed at the Alexandrian policy of colonization. Though they exported Greek language and overlords to their conquered territories, they allowed the indigenous subjects to maintain their local customs and culture. It resulted in a fusion of Greek and Eastern culture.

"How your great emperor keep order in such mixed state of custom?" asked Chang in halted Greek to Balthazar. "If our states were allow such freedom, they return to tribal war."

Balthazar replied, "They are one in language and law under the emperor. But by allowing them to keep their tribal traditions, they are not as likely to rebel. We call those who crush the freedom of the individual, 'tyrants.'"

Chang laughed heartily. "That is a funny sounding word. Tyrant." Sometimes translation between languages created such oddities.

Balthazar noticed the laugh as being out of Chang's eastern character. He was becoming more western in his expressions. Balthazar smiled at the thought of their captive being a kind of chameleon in his ability to adapt so smoothly to his newfound cultural interest. Like the magi, eastern scholars were not as bound by provincial superstitions and prejudices. They were more open because they sought knowledge, and knowledge was salvation from the closed picture of the world that ignorance too often bred.

Chang said, "I check navigation. We are close to destination."

After Chang left, Balthazar locked the door behind him. He moved to the bed and pushed a box aside on the pile of boxes. He pulled the box behind it to the forefront and opened the lid.

Inside the straw lined box were the two sacred relics from the temple; the mysterious golden cup and the magical staff. He cradled the cup and read the ancient Semitic language engraved on the side, "Manna." It was a word that meant, "What is it?" When the Israelites had escaped their slavery to Egypt and were wandering in the desert wilderness, the legend went that their god, Yahweh, would magically provide food for his people. Every morning, a strange flakey substance would appear with the dew of night, like frost on the ground. It was edible, and the Israelites would gather it up daily to eat for their sustenance. But it would rot by the end of the day, requiring them to trust that Yahweh would provide more the next day. At first, they weren't sure what it was, so they called it, "manna" or "what is it" in a humorous nod to their creator and sustainer. The manna in this sealed jar was a special sample of heavenly bread that never rotted, as a miraculous testimony that Yahweh would provide for them forever. He was their "bread of life."

The other relic was the staff of the high priesthood of Aaron. It too had magical properties, at least in its origin. For when Yahweh was proving to the Israelites whose set of priests were his, he had all the tribes set forth a staff. And the staff that miraculously blossomed with almond flowers overnight would be the staff of Yahweh's chosen priesthood. Aaron's rod alone blossomed, thus verifying the exclusive priesthood as belonging to his tribe, the Levites. It had also been used as a symbol of judgment on Pharaoh's house, for when his sorcerers turned their own staffs into serpents, this staff had turned into a serpent that swallowed the other serpents alive, thus showing Yahweh's power over the Serpent and his minions.

When they had received these sacred items in the days of Nebuchadnezzar, it had become the magi's sacred duty for generations to protect the relics with their lives. There is no way Balthazar would risk them in the hands of lesser guardians and he would not risk hiding them, only to have them lost forever if he and his brothers never returned from Tianxia. Of course, they were so insignificant in their appearance that probably no one would recognize their importance should they find them anyway. Unless their magic was released, a magic Balthazar had yet to see and no idea how to call forth.

Oh mighty Marduk of fifty names, he prayed, *please keep your servants Melchior and Gaspar alive wherever they be.*

Balthazar's prayer was interrupted by the distant shout of captain Antiochus on the bridge. "All hands on deck!"

Excitement shot through Balthazar. He hastily repacked the relics, hid them under the straw, and replaced the humble box in the back. He then rushed out of his quarters onto deck.

When Balthazar arrived up top, everyone not rigging ropes or pulling sails was standing in awe at the sight on the port side of their vessel. The shore was lined with beautiful and strange looking trees. A mountain range rose majestically in the deep background. The air was pure and clean, allowing them to see for many miles. Chang was pointing inland toward a mountain on the shoreline and shouting, "Langya! Langya!"

They had been sailing along the coastline of Tianxia for some time. He had told them of the city at Langya, and its entry point into the complex of rivers that would take them inland to the emperor's capital city.

They had already been spotted by the local inhabitants and two ships were making their way toward their vessel as a welcome party. Two very large Ch'inese warships.

CHAPTER 11

The 27th year of the reign of the First Emperor of Tianxia.

The first thing that Antiochus and Balthazar could see of the two warships bearing down upon them was their size and shape. The lead ship was a junk style vessel that Chang had explained to them earlier. It was a flat-bottom boat that rode well on both ocean and river. It was about seventy feet wide and one hundred fifty feet long with multiple large red-ribbed sails that looked like angled fish fins. In contrast, Antiochus' Greek trireme was a thin long ship of two hundred feet but only thirty feet wide with one main square, white sail. The oars were withdrawn because they were not going to battle today. And it appeared that they would not be able to out-sail the speedy boats approaching them.

But what made everyone on the trireme stare was the monstrous super-sized fortress following the lead ship. It looked to be about three hundred feet long and about two hundred feet wide. It was without sails, moving under the power of paddlewheels below the surface instead of oars. Its deck could only be described as a castle. It was a castle on a square boat. It looked like it held over a thousand troops behind its fortified walls manning hundreds of large mounted cross bows. It stayed back like a war hound behind its master, ready to be unleashed. Its size did not appear to hinder its speed. Antiochus imagined a thousand captives in the lower decks paddling for their lives. It was awesome and powerful.

The Greek sailors manned their stations in preparation to receive the Ch'inese warship. In battle, the trireme had a bronze sheathed battering ram in its prow for ramming enemies. But Antiochus had presented its broadside in submission to the approaching battleship. He yelled to his warriors aboard, "Present no arms!" The sailors kept their bows, spears and swords out of sight. They were ostensibly here on a diplomatic mission. Most of them were secretly grateful because a conflict with this foreign warship and its monstrous companion would surely prove disastrous.

Antiochus could now see the general on the prow of the approaching warship. He wore golden plated armor unlike anything Antiochus had ever seen, with a simple smooth golden helmet sporting a red feathered plume. His bright red cloaks beneath the armor were accented with a golden silken cape that flew behind him in the wind.

Chang suddenly belted out in his native language, "General Meng Tian! General Meng Tian!" He waved his hands in the air to draw the attention of the Asian leader.

The General's stern eyes widened with surprise. Chang said to Antiochus in his primitive Greek, "Look. His surprise give him wide round eye like Greek."

Antiochus looked at the smiling Chang, who turned back and yelled in Ch'inese, "I am Chang Shen of the royal court of scholars! Returned from the western lands of Babel!"

Antiochus deliberately allowed Chang unbound freedom in order to affirm their diplomatic intent. Though their goal was hostage exchange, they would have to make the good faith offer of Chang without hostility. They were after all, at the mercy of this eastern empire and its obvious military might.

The Ch'inese general reminded Antiochus of an Asian version of Hermias. He was an older veteran with graying hair and a creased face from years of war experience. Antiochus knew such men were the same, regardless of culture. Pragmatic, focused, not taken to frivolity. Warriors the world over had a certain camaraderie, in spirit if not in politics or ethnicity. Warriors understood one another. He hoped he could make a connection with this brooding leader.

Balthazar recognized the armed soldier beside the Ch'inese general. Compact, intense, relentless. He said, "Chang, who is that, next to the General?"

Chang said, "That is Wu Shu, his champion warrior."

Balthazar whispered to Antiochus, "He was the one at Marduk's temple."

Balthazar had previously told Antiochus of this warrior who had taken out fifteen Seleucid temple guards single-handedly, and kidnapped the magi. He said he fought like an angel of death.

Antiochus smirked, "Well, we know we are in the right place, then."

At that very moment, Balthazar's attention was drawn to the water below their ship. The sight evoked in him both a shiver of fear and an undeniable sense of wonder. He saw a huge scaled serpentine body glide silently below the surface, barely visible in the darkness of the deep. It passed beneath them with long fluid movement. It was huge. It passed and sank smoothly back into the deep like a phantom. Balthazar figured it was three times the size of their own ship. Massive.

And then the sea monster was gone.

He looked back up to see if Antiochus or the others had seen it as well. But everyone had been focused on the members of the opposing vessel, and the tense moment of possible confrontation.

No one else had seen the colossal creature.

Was it a magical protector of these strange mystical people? A secret weapon at their bidding?

A pale of dread came over Balthazar. It was surely an omen of the future.

CHAPTER 12

Antiochus docked his ship at the Langya port. A mountain rose before them with a large tower on it that reached to the heavens. The General had a receiving party arrive from the tower above. Antiochus could see the beginning of the long spiral of steps that led up to the top. But there was also a mechanical elevator that could carry a dozen or more people directly up the precipitous mountainside. He stood on the dock with Balthazar and a few guards. They watched Chang ten feet away talking to the General. They could hear snippets of their dialogue.

Antiochus noticed that the General had his helmet off. His hair was black and long as a woman's, as was that of all the soldiers. Some of it was pulled up into a silly looking knot on the top of his head with huge hair pins in it, allowing the rest of the long locks to lie down around his shoulders. He had learned from Chang that their hair was considered sacred, and an expression of their status. It struck Antiochus as a hindrance for battle.

Balthazar whispered to Antiochus, "Langya is one of the emperor's favorite vacation spots. He keeps a complete retinue of servants and concubines available for visits at any time."

Antiochus was barely listening to him, because he had scanned the entourage of a dozen servants and had noticed a single woman in their midst.

A single vision of heaven.

It was difficult for Antiochus to distinguish most of them because they all looked so similar to him. The same almond-shaped dark eyes, the same long black hair, with the exception that the plebeians apparently tended to have their hair down. But this servant stood out to him like a shining star. She wore the same plain brown woolen robe as the others, but it didn't seem to fit her glowing presence. Her skin was very pale, almost translucent. Her lips were pulpy and her eyes unusually large. But the mark that distinguished her most, that gave her a haunting presence, was a large scar that crossed her left cheek down to her chin. It was like a gash from the gods to keep her beauty from achieving absolute earthly perfection. A reminder of human frailty in the face of a goddess.

But it couldn't stop Antiochus from his worshipful stare.

Balthazar noticed his leader's trance and saw the servant woman staring back, transfixed. Then she suddenly turned and scurried away into the housing structures on the dock. Antiochus was shaken out of his trance.

The Ch'inese General advanced toward Antiochus and Balthazar with Chang at his side, smiling as always.

A guard of eight soldiers followed the General protectively.

He stopped and stood before Antiochus. They were approximately the same height, which was unusual as the rest of the Ch'inese tended to be a foot smaller than the average Greek.

Balthazar wondered why the gods made them so small. Antiochus wondered what their diet consisted of.

The General looked at Antiochus with what appeared to be a stern frown. Chang had warned Antiochus earlier that this was the general's normal look.

Antiochus bowed deferentially as he had been advised to do. It consisted of placing one's arms in a circle in front of them, hands cupped within each other. The General returned the bow and spoke to Antiochus in Ch'inese. Balthazar whispered to him, "He says his name is General Meng Tian and he welcomes you on behalf of the emperor."

Antiochus replied to him, "I am honored to meet you, General. My name is Antiochus the Younger, son of Antiochus the Great, emperor of Seleucia. I am here on a diplomatic mission to your emperor."

Balthazar did his best with Ch'inese to repeat the words to the general. Chang corrected him on some minor pronunciations.

Meng Tian looked at Balthazar with a bit of surprise. He said in Ch'inese, "I am impressed that you have learned a bit of our language."

The General turned and gestured to a large stone monument at the center of the walkway to the stairs. It had an inscription on it. "Do you see this declaration of the emperor? I will read it and your scholar shall translate for all your party to listen and understand."

He gestured for them to follow him to the stele. Antiochus alerted his own guard to follow him. They stood before the monument and Meng Tian read it, with Balthazar translating.

A new age is inaugurated by the Emperor.

Rules and measures are rectified,

The myriad things set in order,

There is harmony between fathers and sons.

The Emperor in his sagacity, benevolence and justice

Has made all laws and principles manifest.

It was typical tyrant drivel to Antiochus. Exaltation of the emperor, his righteousness and compassion, demands for obedience by his subjects, and warnings of punishment for disobedience. Finally, they finished with an ode to his absolute sovereignty.

The universe entire

Is our Emperor's realm,

Wherever human life is found,

All acknowledge his suzerainty,

All creatures benefit from his virtue,

All live in peace at home.

When the General finished, Antiochus saw a tear in his eye. He knew this one was not like Hermias after all. He was a true believer. A man of tradition and loyalty. That could prove to be far more dangerous.

The General said, "The emperor will want to meet you."

CHAPTER 13

Chang stood with Antiochus and Balthazar on the deck of the trireme as it followed the junk ship up the river into the interior. Fortunately, the trireme was shallow enough to navigate the river waters. Antiochus used his oarsmen to paddle upstream. The Ch'inese ship was so constructed that its sail could completely spin around, allowing it to advance directly into the wind without a need for human labors at the oars. Balthazar suspected this was just the beginning of wondrous knowledge he was about to gain from these strange foreigners and their strange ways.

The landscape was as exotic as was the people. They first passed through thick rich jungle forests followed by mountains unlike any they had seen in Mesopotamia or Syria. They rose in multitudes like tall individual piles of rock in the setting sun. They reminded Balthazar of a field of natural ziggurats.

He spotted a most alien creature staring out at their ship as they passed. It appeared to be a bear that was black and white in its color with big black spots around its eyes. Chang told him it was a "panda."

Antiochus muttered under his breath, "So they do exist." He smiled, remembering the story his mother told him of how these peaceful bears gained their spotted black and white coloring. As the fable went, long ago, they were once white. But one day, a shepherdess saved a little panda cub from being attacked by a leopard. In protecting the baby bear, the girl was killed by the large cat. Then at her funeral, all the bears came and put ashes on their fur as was the custom. They rubbed their eyes from crying and held their ears because the mourning had become so loud. The ashes then created the coloring that would mark the bears for the rest of their lives.

The panda watched them from the midst of a forest of tall green, straight skinny trees Chang called "bamboo."

Chang said, "Bamboo is the staff of life. It is food for creatures like the panda and the gorilla. It is considered a noble gentleman in our culture, virtuous, upright, strong and—" Antiochus interrupted him, "And persevering." He was repeating what his mother had told him so many times he could not forget.

Balthazar looked at Antiochus with curiosity. Chang smiled and finished, "Yes, that is correct. We use it for writing, building homes, weapons, and even eating."

Have I run from my future only to face my past? thought Antiochus. *Have I reached the ends of the earth, only to return home?*

The "virtuous" bamboo reminded him of the beautiful woman he had seen at the landing place. He could not stop thinking about her. He could not forget her dangerous beauty.

They were interrupted by the arrival of a sailor announcing, "General Antiochus. We have a stowaway." He crowed proudly, pulling forward a bound woman in a dark robe.

Antiochus saw it was the beautiful servant woman!

"Release her," he huffed.

The sailor was surprised. He had been hoping for some recognition. Instead he was reprimanded.

They retired quickly to Antiochus' cabin, joined by Balthazar and Chang.

Antiochus handed the woman a cup of water. He asked her with his limited Ch'inese, "Who are you?"

She averted her eyes when she spoke. "My name is Mei Li."

Chang added, "She is one of the emperor's concubines."

Antiochus and Balthazar responded with shock.

Antiochus asked Chang, "Then why does she dress as a servant? And why did she stowaway? Is she in trouble?"

Chang did not have to ask her. He knew the answer. "She disdain her station. She has rebellious spirit. In Tianxia, hierarchy must be obeyed. Independence not allowed."

Antiochus could not keep his eyes off of her. He asked, "Why would she spurn such privileged status?"

Chang answered, "She was at Langya because she is out of his favor."

Chang then explained to Mei Li what Antiochus was asking him. Antiochus now knew with certainty that he was in the land of his mother's people. His suspicions had been confirmed. There was something in that beautiful concubine's eyes that carried the mystery of his origins, and he hoped the salvation of his soul.

She spoke in Ch'inese simple enough for Antiochus to follow, "My scar makes me an outcast from the royal palace."

Antiochus saw in her bodily behavior a ritual humility. She would rarely look any of them in the eye. Was she timid or ashamed? But he now felt a strong desire to learn their language, unlike his feelings about it during the entire trip across the sea. He was determined to immerse himself to catch up in his understanding.

"I am sorry for your suffering," said Antiochus.

Mei Li replied, still not looking at him, "Do not be. The emperor ignores me. I can move about freely, so long as I stay out of his way."

Antiochus could not believe it. "But that is cruelty."

"It is my freedom."

Chang added, "Do not be quick to judge."

Antiochus pulled back.

Chang added, "In Tianxia, it would be wrong to allow such blemish in the presence of the perfection of the emperor."

Antiochus knew that their worlds thought differently and treated each other differently. Nevertheless, he could see the self-exaltation of tyrants was the same all over the world. Maybe they were not all that different in their nature after all.

"This emperor of yours acts like a god."

Chang replied, "He is a god."

CHAPTER 14

The journey through five hundred miles of intersecting river systems took them days to navigate before arriving at their destination, which now towered above them on the north side of the River Wei: the imperial city of Xianyang.

The desert rocky terrain in this area was a marked contrast with the lush green forests and mountain jungles they had recently passed through. It seemed as if they entered into a land that had the life sucked out of the ground. In a way, it seemed to match the stoic emotionless character of the Ch'inese Balthazar had already met. Even Chang had reverted back to his expressionless original self, no longer joining in hearty laughter or outward emotion.

Chameleon indeed, thought Balthazar. But he couldn't judge him too harshly for it. It was one way to survive. Scholarly knowledge had a way of diffusing loyalty to anyone or anything other than the hungry pursuit of more knowledge. And the more one learned of worlds outside one's own, the more one learned about ignorance and prejudice and the more one became less able to fanatically support any single world.

They walked through the gates of the towering walls before them and entered into a different world yet again. It was a lively city, full of hardworking peasants carrying water, food and building materials on their shoulders. They were dressed in simple colorless tattered robes, the eastern version of their plebeian western counterparts in Mesopotamia. They passed through markets that sold vegetables and other foods, much of it unrecognizable to the Greek visitors.

The governmental architecture riveted Antiochus and Balthazar. It contained all the imagination and color that seemed lacking in their home city. The color red dominated on colorful buildings with orange tiled roofs that looked like large hats with curled up edges. Chang called this a "pagoda" style. The larger buildings with multiple stories looked like a series of curled pagoda hats placed on top of each level.

Balthazar thought of the square, colorless and lifeless Babylonian living space compared to this bright, organic Ch'inese sensibility for beauty. The wood and earth-packed walls of Tianxia were flexible and alive, the stone of his home Mesopotamia was immovable and lifeless in comparison.

The Imperial Palace was even more outstanding as they entered it. The colorful Ishtar Gate was primitive compared to the intricacies of detail in the gates of this Palace district. Curling flames, flowers and dragons. It was like entering a kind of paradise.

Antiochus led his pared-down crew, surrounded by Meng Tian's soldiers, through a vast, wide open courtyard to the next inner gate of the palace. Hellenic palaces were large, but filled with pillars and cold damp stone architecture. He felt he could breathe easier here, the air itself feeling pure and fresh in his lungs. This new world was enchanting.

They moved through a second gate into new palatial grounds. Balthazar noticed it was laid out like a temple with increasing areas of gated holiness the closer one got to the sanctuary. And the sanctuary stood before them now, at the top of a myriad of steps. The Palace of Ch'in, a massive towering achievement of oriental architecture.

Ascending the steps felt like ascension into heaven itself.

Too bad this god is only a man, thought Balthazar.

Antiochus wondered where the Achilles heel was for this proud despot they were about to meet. When he found it, he would exploit it.

When they reached the top, they could see up close the intricacy of beauty in all its detail. Mammoth multi-leveled sloping pagoda roofs. Bright red pillars. Ornate latticework that looked like hand-carved wooden lace adorning the entire imperial house. It stunned the Greeks. All of them.

And yet, it was strangely familiar to Antiochus. As if he had been here before, but only in his dreams—dreams that were fueled by his mother's exotic fairy tales of distant adventure and romance. Those dreams now came alive before his eyes with wonder.

They entered the palace.

Two fighters clashed with staffs before the royal throne as entertainment. One of them was Wu Shu, the champion of the emperor.

His taut, sinewy form moved gracefully, effortlessly, like a cobra toying with its prey.

His prey was Fusu, the eldest royal son of the emperor. Over twenty years of age, well built, and practiced, Fusu was still no match for his master. His powerful thrusts and strong attacks were easily diverted and turned against him by Wu Shu.

Antiochus sat transfixed by the fighting style. It was alien and exotic, yet strangely poetic, like a ballet. He wanted to understand its principle, the philosophy behind the power. He thought again of the dangerous beauty that seemed to typify much of this entire Asian cosmos.

Balthazar was more entranced by the throne room. He kept glancing around at the vast hall. Soldiers lined up along the huge pillars. They held artistically designed glaives, large menacing blades at the end of a pole. The Greek arrival party sat on the floor facing the throne, and between visitors and host, the current sparring went on.

On either side, an assortment of scholars, royalty and other advisors watched the combat display, sitting perfectly still, some with pin-bunned hair, others with tightly fit hats, all with flowing robes and hidden hands.

The throne was particularly exalting. Balthazar read the large banners hanging on red pillars as best he could. *Emperor of all under heaven.*

Everything upon the throne was adorned with paintings, engravings and tapestries of fluid-looking curlicues, flowers and serpentine dragons. The Ch'inese dragons were not like the western conception of a full bodied reptilian behemoth. They were more like long twisting and writhing snakes with small legs. Western notions of dragons involved fire, these Eastern ones involved water.

A few advisors and royal members stood beside the throne dressed in shimmering, flowing black fabric with bright accents of blue, red and gold dragons. The sleeves of their robes expanded like hanging waterfalls of smooth fabric. Chang had described the shiny material to them as "silk." It was made from web-like material created by special worms. It made the wearers seem otherworldly to Balthazar. And black seemed to be their royal color as purple was for the Seleucids. Most of their hair was pinned up in buns or knots with elaborate ornate carved head pieces and huge hair pins.

The emperor sat on the throne with his proud chin angled high, looking down on the sport from his lofty perch. He looked about forty years old, and sported a thin mustache with beard on his lower chin. His robe was bright blue and full of golden dragons and flowing ornate designs. He wore a special crown that held a series of strings in front of his face and behind his head. Small golden beads were threaded through the strings to partially obscure the ruler's face. Chang had explained to them that this crown represented the stars of heaven, deities among whom the emperor resided.

Balthazar had been amazed at how similar their own understanding of astral deities were. They too considered the stars interchangeable with the gods who ruled the nations of the earth. Although in the Hellenic world, astralization or apotheosis of the king would only happen after their death, as they would ascend to the stars to become gods. This king evidently considered himself already divine. Balthazar wondered how long it would be before Greek kings would claim the same prerogatives of divinity.

Antiochus noticed a twitch in the emperor's face as if a sharp pain afflicted his skull. Apparently, the divinity was not beyond the pain of an earthly headache. The emperor waved his hand.

Meng Tian clapped his hands loudly.

The warriors on the floor stopped instantly. They bowed to each other.

The emperor said to the lesser fighter, "Well done, my son. You are an accomplished fighter. I am impressed with your training. Now if I could only have Li Ssu train you to rid yourself of that love of Confucius, you would be fit to succeed the throne. Come, stand by your brother."

Fusu bowed and stepped up to the throne to stand beside a smaller, younger, and softer sibling. Wu Shu knelt down beside Meng Tian.

Meng Tian stood with Antiochus and Chang as his interpreter. They approached the throne and bowed, hands interlocked before their bodies.

Meng Tian said, "Your divine majesty, I present to you General Antiochus the Younger from Seleucia at the western ends of the earth."

The emperor remained distant and unemotional in his gaze upon the foreigners.

The closest advisor stepped forward. He was graying, and wore the white robes and black scarf sashes of the scholars. He had calculating eyes. The most like a serpent of all of them.

He spoke and Chang translated. "Welcome to the court of his majesty Ch'in Shih Huang Di, the first august emperor of all under heaven, god on earth."

Antiochus bowed in response. They had been learning the rules of propriety from Chang, who now muttered to him, "That is Li Ssu, his Chancellor, the highest post in the kingdom." Chang had told them about this man on their sea voyage. He was an adherent to a new philosophy called Legalism and he promoted it passionately. He had advised the emperor to institute harsh legal reforms that conflicted with their Confucian traditions. Confucius taught feudal values of family loyalty, ancestor worship and respect for elders. That emphasis on the family as the primary foundation of good government did not comport well with an absolute monarch and an all-powerful state.

Chang whispered, "The two younger men beside the emperor are his sons, Fusu and Huhai, the crown princes." Fusu was the fighter, Huhai, the younger, looked bookish and intellectual.

Li Ssu said, "Chang Shen, I see you have learned the westerners' language."

"Yes, my chancellor."

"Good. We shall not be barbarians to one another." The word barbarian was a reference to the fact that foreigners spoke gibberish that sounded like "bar bar bar."

Antiochus spoke to the emperor with Chang's help. "I represent my emperor of Seleucia. His kingdom in the west is as large as yours is in the east. And I bring you a gift. Your scholar, wounded but healed by my magi."

Chang bowed at the reference to himself. The emperor glared at Antiochus silently.

Antiochus added, "I am sure you know of the circumstances, as your warrior, Wu Shu here, has no doubt attested to." Antiochus had tactfully and politely implied his knowledge of the mercenary mission to kidnap the magi.

Antiochus decided to damn this indirectness and spoke out clearly to the emperor, "He is an offering of diplomacy—in exchange for the magi you now hold hostage."

Li Ssu waved his hand. A slew of guards stepped forward and surrounded them with a fence of dagger-axes pointing directly at them. These were imperial pole weapons whose heads were shaped like both a dagger and an axe.

Li Ssu continued to speak for his ruler. "An 'emperor' of the West, you claim?"

Antiochus said, "As his majesty is emperor of the East."

Li Ssu laughed. "The East? Tianxia is the central kingdom. It is all under heaven. It has no boundaries."

"Nevertheless," said Antiochus, "the emperor sent secret forces to do his bidding in my sovereign's territory."

The emperor finally spoke out. He looked amused. "You pale round-eyed descendants of Cyrus retain his pride and stubbornness as well."

Antiochus immediately switched his attention to the ruler. "My intentions are not hostile, my lord. I returned Chang Shen in good faith to you, not in aggression. I came in a single vessel, not an armada. I am at your mercy."

The emperor smiled. "Indeed, you are.

"I am afraid I must reject your offer. You see, I need your magi."

Antiochus' heart sank.

"But I will return them."

There is hope, thought Antiochus.

"*After* they have helped me find the elixir of immortality."

Elixir of immortality? Antiochus mused. *And I thought my king was mad.*

Behind him, Balthazar felt dread come over him. He knew what was coming next.

The emperor added, "And I am afraid I will need your other magus to help them."

The guards grabbed Balthazar. Antiochus drew his sword. The dozen dagger-axes closed to within inches of his head, throat and heart. He sheathed his weapon.

The guards led Balthazar out of the throne room.

The emperor said, "I apologize for my aggression, General Antiochus. Please, let me make it up to you. You are welcome to wait for your magi. I will appoint an escort to show you the wonders of Tianxia during your wait. You may travel freely within my empire."

He waved and the guards withdrew their pole arms.

Right, thought Antiochus. *Within your empire.*

Just then, one of the bowing servants of the entourage stepped forward and stood beside Antiochus. The guards closed in again.

Antiochus gaped. It was Mei Li.

She said, "Allow me to escort the foreigners, my lord."

The emperor appeared surprised, confused. Antiochus could see Li Ssu's face flushed with anger. But Mei Li stared back at the emperor, small, defiant—beautiful as a dream to Antiochus.

The emperor's surprise turned into a smile. Antiochus thought it looked like a gaming smile, as if she had won a round of dice by tricking him. He wagged his finger at the little woman.

"Mei Li, you continue to prove yourself an untamable tigress."

She bowed. "A tigress on the open range is far from the master's abode, is she not, my lord?"

The emperor laughed again, and said, "Your request is granted."

Mei Li bowed.

Antiochus tried to figure out what just happened. But he could see Li Ssu was not happy.

"One more thing," added the emperor. He turned to his left and waved at some guards by the pillared walls.

They pulled out a shackled prisoner and dragged him over before the throne, mere yards from Antiochus and Mei Li.

"This is General Wei," said the emperor. "He led the expeditionary force to Babylon."

General Wei had his back to the emperor, and was facing Antiochus with a kind of stoic look.

The emperor finished, "He was not supposed to kidnap your magi. He was supposed to offer them gold and silver freely."

He gave a guttural yelp, some kind of an order.

Wu Shu raised a huge scimitar sword and swung it around with a mighty force at Wei's neck.

Antiochus watched in horror as the head fell to the marble floor and rolled to Antiochus' feet.

The emperor said with a sudden lightheartedness, "My gesture of good faith to you, General Antiochus. May we grow in each other's trust."

Antiochus remained silent. He couldn't tell if it was proof of the emperor's apology or a veiled threat.

Maybe it was both.

CHAPTER 15

Chang brought Balthazar under guard to the south part of the royal palace. The magus looked up at the structure and read the banner aloud, "Academy of Scholars."

"Yes," said Chang. "We must get you proper robes before I introduce you."

Chang brought him to a changing room where Balthazar took off his Greek garb and donned a black robe with white sash and scarf, the opposite of the colors of the scholars. *It must be the garb of forced servitude,* thought Balthazar.

The Academy had its own structure with several floors. When he walked in the entrance, Balthazar noted it was much less ornamental than the royal palace. More functional. Scholars were, as magi were, more interested in knowledge than beauty.

Chang told him, "There are four hundred and fifty scholars congregated here for the emperor. They are divided by fields of study such as alchemy, astronomy, medicine, divination, agriculture, poetry, history, and philosophy. But we live together."

Balthazar was shown his sleeping quarters, a communal arrangement with a monkish lifestyle.

Then he arrived at a room guarded by bronze doors carved with images of dragons and magic. Chang paused and said to him with pride, "The alchemist's laboratory. Where scholar and magician work together."

He passed the guards and pushed the doors open.

Inside, Balthazar saw a workplace not too different from his own alchemy lab in Babylon. It was filled with dozens of scholars and magicians scattered around the large room engaged in various activities of cutting and combining, melting and mixing herbs and elements, all in the search of the perfect prescription. Strange devices, containers of materials, and at the back of the room, a double furnace with massive doors emanating heat through the entire lab. This was not a heating stove, but rather an oven used in the process of their sciences. The magicians could be differentiated from the white-robed scholars by their black robes with white sashes just like Balthazar.

A familiar voice called out, "Balthazar!"

Two black-robed magicians came running at him, one tall and thin, the other smaller and stout.

"Melchior! Gaspar!"

The three magi collided in a trio of embrace.

Gaspar said, "I told you he would come for us."

Melchior said, "You did not. You said he would never find us."

"Yes, but that meant he would be looking for us."

"Gaspar, that is not what you meant."

"So, now you are a reader of minds?"

"Quiet, you two," said Balthazar. But then he smiled. "On second thought, bicker away. It is long-lost music to my ears."

They laughed and hugged one another tighter.

Balthazar pulled away and looked at Gaspar in his outfit. "So, I see they are feeding you well for your efforts."

Gaspar smiled. "They have the most exotic of delicacies you can imagine! Sea creatures that will astound your taste buds! Their bread is called 'rice' and they grow it in huge fields of water. We eat it with everything. They even make wine from it."

Balthazar smiled. "Unfortunately, I understand the only drink the emperor is interested in is an elixir of immortality."

The other two became sober.

"From what I can see of this emperor's determination, if we do not help these scholars and magicians to come up with it, you two will not have each other to squabble with anymore."

The two brothers noticed Chang. Balthazar said, "This is Chang Shen, the one left for dead at Babylon."

They exchanged bows with hands firmly clasped before them. Gaspar said, "He wasn't there when we were fighting."

"We were not the only ones fighting, moron," said Melchior. He changed the subject, "Does he understand our Greek?"

"Better than I do his Ch'inese."

Melchior said, "We have learned it from necessity."

Balthazar added, "He has been quite a help to us. I think he is a Hellenist at heart. He is enraptured with Aristotle."

The brothers smiled.

Chang spoke in Greek with sad eyes, "I humbly apologize for your inconvenience. The emperor has punished the general who kidnapped you for his disobedience."

Balthazar drew his finger across his throat. "They were supposed to bribe you."

Chang pulled in close and whispered, "But do not believe everything the emperor tells you."

The three looked at each other with surprise. Perhaps they had an ally in this fellow scholar.

The lead magician approached them, an intense fifty five-year old man with a long beard and penetrating eyes. Magicians wore colorful robes with swirling patterns. Anything to promote their mystery and esoteric arts.

Chang said, "This is Xu Fu, the chief magician." He turned to Xu Fu. "This is Balthazar, their chief of magicians they call magi."

They exchanged more bows and Xu Fu said, "Then we are fellow scholars and magicians united across worlds. Please take time and introduce your fellow magus to our processes." He pulled Chang aside to discuss some pressing issues.

Melchior took over with excitement. "You will never believe this, Balthazar. Their knowledge is not that different from our own."

Gaspar interrupted like an excited child. "They have astrology just like us, but their medicine is different. They stick needles into their body to cure diseases!"

"Gaspar," complained Melchior. "Will you please let me finish?"

"Sorry."

Melchior said, "We'll talk about the astrology later. But regarding this elixir of immortality, they have some strange ideas. First off, their base elements of the cosmos are somewhat different than ours. Where we have four: earth, wind, fire and water, they have five; earth, water, fire, wood and metal. But they too believe in the unity of heaven and earth. They call it the Tao. It means, "The Way," and it is the life force that is embedded in all things and connects all things in oneness."

Gaspar blurted out, "Tell him about yin and yang."

Melchior glared at Gaspar. "Well, why don't you just tell him, since you seem so intent upon stealing my thunder, mighty mumbling Marduk?"

Gaspar jumped at the chance. "All right. The yin and yang are the complementary principles that—"

Now Melchior interrupted, "On second thought, I better finish it or you will confuse Balthazar with your excursions into observational minutia."

Gaspar frowned. Melchior continued. "The yin and yang are complementary principles that create all reality. They are opposites that transform into one another. Yin signifies the passive female and yang signifies the active male. Alchemy is turning an element into its opposite. Yin into yang, or vice versa."

Balthazar could see the various stations of scientists melting or burning some elements with small flames, others mixing them with liquids to dissolve. Still others crushing and mashing herbs and other substances together.

Balthazar said, "This is all quite similar to our Hermetic tradition from Egypt."

"Exactly," said Melchior. "But with some differences. Come over here."

He dragged Balthazar over to a large container of reddish brown earth. He grabbed a handful of it. "This is cinnabar. They believe it to be the sacred opposite of quicksilver and gold, both life-giving elements. If consumed in tiny doses, they believe both will bring longevity, if too big a dose, it brings death. They have used smelting to transform it into quicksilver, but have not achieved gold."

Balthazar said, "The philosopher's stone."

 The other two magi nodded with agreement.

The philosopher's stone was the western tradition's concept for the same pursuit of turning base metals like lead into artificial drinkable gold that would bring about not only enlightenment and wisdom but immortality.

Balthazar asked, "How do they test their prescriptions?"

Melchior said with a hush, "On unwitting slaves, I'm afraid."

Gaspar added darkly, "Many have died."

Balthazar saw a man in a strange-looking puffy suit that covered his entire body like a big mitt. He approached the fiery furnace to withdraw some stone pots with liquefied elements in them.

Gaspar said, "That man is wearing a strange fibrous substance that is impervious to the flames and can protect them from the heat. Their experiments have yielded many such accidents of discovery."

Melchior said, "Xu Fu has achieved only mild success with quicksilver, sulfur and arsenic. He believes these can extend the emperor's life, so they are feeding him tiny amounts of all three."

Gaspar smiled deviously. "But the emperor is not getting younger, he is getting sicker. He suffers from migraines, tremors, nausea, and rashes."

Melchior added, "Xu Fu believes those are signs that his mortality is leaving him."

Balthazar grinned with pleasure. "Well, then by all means, let us continue the treatment."

CHAPTER 16

Antiochus awakened in his guest room. It was decorated as the rest of the palace was, a large bed with canopy on poles carved with dragons and fluid characters of unknown stories. Wooden carved lattices, marble floor, gold handles, exotic tapestries, ornamentation on everything. It was like living inside a fable, surrounded by story and image.

He washed, and dressed in robes provided by their host. It felt strange at first, but it began to grow on him.

He was brought to the palace gardens where Mei Li, his escort, awaited him. She bowed. "Good morning, General Antiochus."

She was no longer dressed as a servant. She was lovely in a red satin robe, her hair partly lying on her shoulders and partly pinned up into the headdress. She still averted her gaze from him. The morning sun shone on her like a goddess in the garden.

The lone figure of Wu Shu stood behind her, dressed in full armor and weapons. He stared forward emotionless, uninvolved, ever vigilant.

Antiochus said in his stunted Ch'inese, "Our guest for today?"

Mei Li bowed. "I have known Wu Shu for many years. He is very capable as bodyguard."

Antiochus said, "From what I have seen of his skill, he is all we need."

Wu Shu remained still and staring as a stone statue.

Antiochus' attention was drawn from Wu Shu to the wondrous display of plants and other foliage that rose around him like a jungle. Everywhere, green, with explosions of flowers of every color. All arranged in a geometric labyrinth for strolling. He thought, *Is this what the hanging gardens of Babylon may have looked like?*

It was truly a garden of the gods, and he saw stone and wooden images on the grounds to verify that thought. Ancestral deities of different names than their western counterparts, but no doubt similar in ultimate identity.

She said, "Our first trip will be a boat ride on the River Wei."

They boarded an imperial junk ship with Wu Shu and floated downriver to the east.

Antiochus looked upon the Imperial City receding in the background. His mind returned to Babylon on the river Euphrates. For the first time in all these months he felt homesick.

He said to her, "In the west, if a concubine or wife approached the king's throne as you did last night, without being summoned, it could result in death."

"It is the same in this kingdom."

"Why then did the emperor not execute you? Is it not an excuse he would happily entertain?"

"Punishing me would bring him shame."

They were approaching a new city being built just downriver.

Antiochus looked at her scar. "He did that to you."

At that moment, It occurred to him that he might have overstepped his bounds, especially in earshot of the emperor's high guard, Wu Shu. Though staunchly disciplined, the Asian warrior's obedience did not render him deaf.

Antiochus glanced at the quiet sentry, whose stoic glare was sullied by unmistakable sorrow. He must be emotionally attached to this concubine. Antiochus now knew something about the warrior that he hoped would prove useful.

Mei Li changed the subject. "This city we are approaching is called Xin Palace. The emperor is building replicas of all the conquered states along the Wei River. There are as many as three hundred in various stages of construction."

Antiochus pulled Mei Li away from the ears of Wu Shu at the other end of the boat. He had decided to take a risk. "I want to tell you something."

She listened intently. He said, "I too was rejected by my king."

She looked confused. "What do you mean?"

"I am his bastard child with the only woman he ever loved. But she was forbidden. A slave." He would not tell her from where. "So I was hidden from the king as a child. When I discovered who I really was, I determined to force the king to accept me as his own. I became a general in his army, and one day I sought to achieve distinction by disobeying his order. It resulted in the death of all my soldiers."

She could see his eyes were filled with pain.

"But it did achieve my desired result. He discovered who I was."

She understood now. And he could see that her eyes were wet with empathy. She said with resignation, "One must sacrifice power to achieve love."

He said, "Or sacrifice love to achieve power. His generals would have mutinied if he did not execute me, regardless of my blood ties. But when your people kidnapped our magi, it gave the king an idea. He faked my execution and sent me here to negotiate release, establish diplomatic connection between our nations, and thereby redeem myself."

He could not tell her the whole truth. The truth about his dragon quest.

She said, "What will he do when you return?"

"I do not know."

She paused thoughtfully and said, "You have more in common with the emperor than you know."

"What do you mean?"

She could not tell him without causing grave danger to them both. "That is for another time and place."

The boat pulled over to a dock on the south bank of the river. Antiochus saw a huge mountain in the distance.

"That is Mount Li," she said. "Follow me, I want to show you something."

They walked their horses from the river down a worn road, followed by Wu Shu, who kept a distance.

Antiochus felt as if an angel walked beside him. She glided over the road like silk. She moved and spoke with elegance and grace.

They broke through into a large clearing and Antiochus stopped, his breath taken away by the sight before him.

A huge ziggurat rested in the valley of the foothills of Mount Li, its top reaching to the heavens.

Mei li said, "That is the tomb of the emperor. He began building it when he came into power. He will be buried in it when he dies." She added with irony, "If he does not find the elixir."

It must have been five hundred feet high, and over fifteen hundred feet square. An entire walled city of hundreds of thousands of builders and workers surrounded the cosmic mountain tomb. There were troops' quarters for guarding the edifice, homes for laborers, and large brick-making pits, all within the several mile radius of the small tomb city.

"Magnificent," gasped Antiochus. "We have the exact same structure in Babylon."

This looked just like the ziggurat Etemenanki with its step pyramid design. A long stairway led up to an altar on the top.

It all began to make sense to Antiochus. He remembered Balthazar's explanation of the Ch'inese word for "tower." It was a picture of the story of the Tower of Babel and the confusion of tongues and the separation of the nations. The Ch'inese must have returned to Babylon to retrieve the ancient wisdom of the tower that they thought the magi would help them find: the elixir of immortality. Ch'in Shih Huang Di had replicated the tower in some kind of desperate bid for eternal life. It was one massive display of hope against the impossible. But the words of Aeschylus the Greek poet echoed in Antiochus' thoughts. "Once a man dies and the earth drinks up his blood, there is no resurrection."

Why then, did her presence resuscitate his weary soul? Her beauty proved the existence of heaven to him, the existence of the divine. He had doubted the gods for so long, but now in this exotic world with this alien woman of such splendor, he felt a sense of transcendence growing in him.

He said to her, "In Babylon, the temple tower is used to worship the gods."

"The emperor does so here as well." She glanced behind them at Wu Shu. He was at a distance, but not far enough away. She leaned close to whisper to him, "But it was not always this way in our land."

"What do you mean?" he whispered back.

She said, "When the emperor unified all under heaven, he changed many things. Some for the better. Some for the worse. He has unified all currencies in the kingdom, as well as weights and measures. He has unified the language as well. These are all good for trade and economy. He has constructed great canal projects for the conservation of water, and he is building a Long Wall in the north to keep out the barbarians. He has brought change with new ways." She gave a nervous glance in Wu Shu's direction. "But he has also brought new gods."

"New gods?" he asked.

She said, "You must not tell the emperor where I am about to take you."

• • • • •

Balthazar entered the library of the Scholar's Academy carrying a collection of papyrus and leather skin scrolls he had stowed in his luggage. He plopped them down upon a table. He knelt down with Melchior and Gaspar and began to open some of them. Chang examined a papyrus scroll with curiosity.

Gaspar was gleeful. "Thank the gods you brought your alchemy texts. Any astrological omina?" *Omina* were texts for interpreting omens.

Balthazar said, "I filled my compartment in the ship with as many as I could."

"Wonderful!" Gaspar and Melchior went through them as well.

Chang could not get over the strange scroll in his hands. "What is this material?"

Gaspar said, "Papyrus. It originated in Egypt and is made from interlocking layers of a reed that grows in marshes." He gestured the interlocking with his fingers.

Melchior mumbled, "Know it all."

Chang said, "May I bring this to our chief magician Xu Fu to analyze? We have been working on something that will be lighter than bamboo that we might mass produce."

Balthazar said, "Bring it to him. We will explain the process later."

Chang left them alone, transfixed by the scroll material. He walked headlong into the door with a loud bump.

Gaspar chuckled.

Melchior muttered, "Do not be so pleased in the misfortune of others, brother."

"Brother," responded Gaspar, "you have no sense of humor."

Melchior ignored him. "We have no sense of how to create the elixir of immortality. I know all our alchemist texts, Balthazar. We have nothing but failure in our attempt to transmute lead into gold. What can we possibly offer these scholars and magicians?"

"We are doubling their ignorance," added Gaspar. "At least, I know Melchior is."

Melchior gave him an angry look.

Balthazar looked about and whispered, "I brought the relics in the ship."

Melchior and Gaspar were not sure what they just heard. Gaspar was the first to respond. "You what?"

"Clear out your ears," said Melchior. He leaned in to Balthazar and hissed, "Balthazar, you jeopardize our holy calling."

Balthazar sat stone-faced. "The magi have watched over the relics for centuries."

Now Gaspar leaned in to their tight circle of whispering. "You could have buried them."

Balthazar said, "If we never returned, they would be lost forever."

Melchior said, "If they find out, they will kill us and they will be lost forever."

Balthazar said, "That is why we must continue to fulfill our duty of guardianship. We must keep them from getting into the wrong hands."

Gaspar said, "There are a lot of wrong hands around here. That may be more difficult than you had planned."

CHAPTER 17

Antiochus watched Mei Li from a distance as she spoke with Wu Shu privately. He could see the stone-faced guardian listening. When she finished, he looked troubled to Antiochus. But after his hesitation, he bowed to the concubine, mounted his horse and left them.

As she returned to Antiochus, she said, "Wu Shu will wait at the boat for us."

There was only one way she could possibly get the guard dog of the emperor to engage in such a violation of his clear duty to shadow them.

"He is in love with you," said Antiochus.

She said nothing. He helped her up on her horse, and mounted his own. But before they moved on, she said sadly, "Wu Shu was an orphan who became a eunuch warrior in the Ch'in elite guard. It was there I met him."

Eunuchs were castrated servants of royalty. It was the only way they could be completely trusted around the palace, and in their death defying missions for the emperor. Without the hope of love, such men became beasts of war. But in Wu Shu's case, some of that humanity remained hidden beneath his soulless eyes of devotion.

She said to him, "Follow me."

They galloped down the path through the woods.

As much as he appreciated the beauty of the scenery around him, the winding, flowing river, the lush green forest, the lofty mountains, none of it was as lovely or as lofty as this exquisite woman riding beside him at this moment. Her hair flowed like a river of silk. Even her riding posture seemed to defy gravity. Now that he was alone with her, he felt himself rising with desire.

They took a path off the main road that led them to a large walled complex about a half mile square. There were no inhabitants, the gates were wide open. Untended vines climbed the walls.

They entered the gate and Antiochus saw a huge field with a ceremonial layout of structures. It was all overrun by weeds and vines from apparent years of disuse. They got off their horses.

Antiochus saw various buildings at the perimeter, but the grounds were open fields more than anything. It felt like sacred space. In the center of the square rose a circular wall surrounding a circular mound of ascending platforms, four of them, that rose fifty feet into the air. It was some kind of ceremonial amphitheater. It gave Antiochus an ethereal feeling of spirituality as the standing stones cast long, ghostly shadows in the setting sun.

He said, "What is this place?"

She answered, "An Altar of Heaven. It is a place of sacrifice to Shang Di."

"Who is Shang Di?"

"He is the one true god. My people worshipped him for thousands of years, since primeval days."

"Apparently, not anymore," he said, noting the unkempt overgrown foliage all around.

She stared off into the distance. "In the time of the warring states, every province had its own altar complex. The king of each state was considered a Son of Heaven who carried the Mandate from Heaven. Once a year, he would perform a 'Border Sacrifice,' on behalf of his people. Sheep and goats were offered up as blood atonement for the people. The largest Altar of Heaven is in Yanjing up north, built by the Zhou dynasty."

She had slipped into a nostalgic mood, staring out as she recounted with loving memory. "The king would purify himself as high priest of Shang Di. He would fast for three days and wash his body clean. Sacrificial animals, usually a goat or lamb, spotless and without blemish, would be drawn from the pens over there." She pointed to a corner of the complex where fences now stood broken and scattered.

She waved at the large circular altar in the center. "That was where the king would sacrifice to heaven—to Shang Di, God most high. All the other gods and spirits would worship him as well."

Antiochus looked around. "I see no images of Shang Di."

"Shang Di is spirit. Images are forbidden."

Antiochus was struck with curiosity. "One true God, no images. There is only one other deity I have ever heard of like that. The god of the Hebrews in Judea. They call him *Yahweh*."

She repeated the name, "Yahweh."

Every other religion across the face of the earth had images of their gods. Zeus in Greece, Isis and Osiris in Egypt, Ahura Mazda in Persia, Shiva, Vishnu and Shakti in India. It was an odd coincidence that these two religions alone forbade images. Was there some connection between them?

"What happened, Mei Li?"

"When the emperor came to power, he abolished the worship of Shang Di. He replaced our ancient tradition with new gods, the inferior gods. He persecuted the old priesthood. The priests of Shang Di, seventy in all, ten from each kingdom, fled for their lives into hiding. If the emperor finds them, he will kill them all."

"Why did he do this?"

Mei Li did not answer immediately. Antiochus could tell she was deciding whether she would tell him or not.

She finally looked straight at him and said, "The emperor is ruled by the Dragon."

Antiochus' mouth went dry. He had sought to keep his true motives for being here a secret. He had kept his eyes open and his ears alert. This was the first reference he had heard the entire time he had been here. He tried to sound more curious than desperate.

He said simply, "Dragon?"

Mei Li said, "The Dragon helped him to subdue the warring states of the six other kingdoms under his own power. Now, he is the Dragon's slave."

Something in Antiochus let go. This woman, this beautiful, mysterious vision had captured his heart. He could not hide from her anymore. He had to risk all. He had to trust her with his life.

"Mei Li, that is the true reason I am here. To capture a dragon and bring it back to my king."

She looked at him with shock. Then she looked away. "I am afraid you do not know the power of the Dragon."

"Then help me."

She stood for a long moment considering his words. Then she said simply, "Maybe we can help each other."

She looked into his eyes for the longest moment, and he could no longer control himself. He moved toward her.

He could see her trembling.

He kissed her.

She responded with the desperation of forbidden desire.

But then, just as suddenly, she withdrew from him and turned away.

He pleaded with her, "Have I shamed you?"

"No. It is I who am shameful."

"Nonsense," he said.

"I do not want your pity."

"Mei Li."

She said nothing.

"Look at me," he begged.

Slowly, she turned her head, trying to keep the scarred left side of her face away from him.

He reached out and tenderly straightened her face toward him. Her scar was in full view.

He said, "Better a diamond with a flaw than a stone without."

She narrowed her eyes at him. She assumed he had learned Confucian sayings from Chang. He would not reveal to her that it was from his mother.

She retorted, "Honeyed words and flattering looks seldom speak of love."

He would not back down. "Wheresoever you go, go with all your heart."

Then he turned her head gently to the right so that her scarred cheek was all he could see.

"I do not pity you. I worship you."

He moved slowly up to her face and kissed the scar. And again. He traced the scar down her face with soft tender kisses that melted her soul.

She surrendered to him.

With all her heart.

CHAPTER 18

The morning rays of the rising sun made the entire countryside glow in the cool of morning. The emperor looked out over the city and its surroundings from the heights of the imperial palace penthouse.

Antiochus joined him. From this vantage point, he saw twelve colossal bronze statues, twenty feet high each, stationed around the exterior of the city, pointing outward. They wore fur skins, conical hats, and bore swords and maces.

"What are those?"

The emperor spoke with pride. "I melted down the weapons of my victory over the seven kingdoms and had those created as totems to guard the city from the *Juren*."

"What are Juren?"

"Giants."

Antiochus remained silent.

"We call them the offspring of the gods. I have put much money and labor into building a Long Wall on the northern perimeter of my empire, a great wall, to keep them out—along with the barbarian hordes. But as we both know, walls are no guarantee of permanent protection."

Huang Di looked at Antiochus' stare. "What is the matter, do you not have giants in Seleucia?"

Antiochus said, "In our myths and legends. They were great titans who were imprisoned in the underworld because of their rebellion."

"Oh, these are not legends, my dear Greek. I can assure you of that." He changed the subject, "Are you pleased with Mei Li?"

Antiochus was thrown by the question. It seemed calculated. He said, "She is an excellent teacher of your ways."

"And are *you* an excellent teacher of *your* ways?"

Antiochus was not sure how to take the remark. Did he mean his cultural ways? Did he suspect their love? Was he stalking him as a tiger would its prey? Wu Shu must have discerned more than Antiochus had hoped, and had informed the emperor.

Antiochus tried to throw him off the scent. "Our nations have much to learn from each other."

The emperor said, "One more than the other."

Antiochus thought the height of this tower reinforced the godlike condescension that corrupted this small man's soul. All people were playthings to such rulers.

The emperor continued, "So I would like to ask you a question. To ascertain the wisdom of your western philosophy."

Antiochus said, "I will do my best to meet your expectations."

The emperor smiled. Antiochus saw him hesitate and cringe just slightly. Another hidden moment of internal pain, headache or other, he wasn't sure.

The emperor proceeded. "I have two sons, as you have seen. My eldest, Fusu, is a strong warrior and leader. He has the traits of a good emperor who would rule justly. And tradition says that he should succeed me. But Fusu is also a loyal follower of Confucius' ideals that stress family, tradition and ancient wisdom. This is a philosophy I have outlawed because it was part of a long period of warring states in Tianxia, whose bloodshed and lawless disorder I alone was able to overcome with my empire."

Antiochus listened carefully. He didn't remember hearing any stories of warring states from his mother. It must have occurred after her people made contact with Cyrus the Great over Babylon. Huang Di paused and stared out over the city with godlike transcendence.

"My youngest son, Huhai, is a weak-minded child. He is easily manipulated, and shows no talent for leadership. But he is a devoted loyal student of Legalism, which I have instituted, and which stresses law, uniformity, and the future. Legalism has produced peace from war, restored unity, identity, and harmony under law."

Antiochus knew what the question would be.

"Now, my dilemma. Should I choose family and tradition and support Fusu's claim to the throne, I would be supporting the very philosophy against which I have sought to rule. I would jeopardize my empire with a return to feudalism, but under a good and just leader." He paused thoughtfully. "Should I choose philosophy and ideals and entrust the throne to Huhai, I would ensure the continuance of Legalism and the Ch'in empire, but at the hands of an incompetent fool and puppet who will no doubt end in ruin. Which son, then would you recommend I choose to succeed me on the throne of my great empire?"

Antiochus said, with resignation, "Good men are rarely great men."

The emperor smiled. "You sound suspiciously like Confucius or Lao Tzu."

Antiochus said, "And what do your advisors say?"

"Li Ssu, my high chancellor, tutors my son Huhai. Meng Tian, my decorated general, has taken Fusu under his wing. Their recommendations are obvious. Without Li Ssu, I would not have my laws, without Meng Tian, I would not have my power. Both are necessary to rule."

Antiochus said, "And if you discover your elixir of immortality, your dilemma resolves itself."

Huang Di replied, "Now you are sounding like a Legalist."

Antiochus returned his smile with an uncomfortable one of his own. This was not an easy predicament to solve. He knew his answer would determine his trustworthiness in the emperor's eyes. He decided to be true rather than calculating.

He sighed deeply. "Well, your majesty, my own king of Seleucia once had a dilemma of his own that was quite similar. His first born was a bastard, the fruit of true love, but not of tradition. His other son was legitimate heir to the throne according to tradition, but only tradition. For he was a cruel son who the king knew would not reign justly. If the king acknowledged his true first born, his dynasty would no doubt dissolve over time and lose power in the eyes of his subjects. If he ignored the bastard child, his dynasty would continue, but only at the expense of justice. Who do you think the king chose?"

Huang Di said, "I might imagine that the king would choose a compromise. Send his first born off on a mission to prove himself and achieve the power he so desperately requires for respect. If the first born fails, the decision is made for the king."

The emperor paused. Antiochus felt his whole body freeze. Did he know about Antiochus' own situation? Was he playing with him?

The emperor smirked. "You are here for dragons."

Antiochus stopped breathing.

He knew. This dangerous madman knew. And there was only one person who could have told him. Everything Antiochus believed about Mei Li, everything he thought was real, came crashing down on him like a wall of bricks. He had thought he had just experienced redemption in her embrace, resurrection even. But it was a trap of death that ensnared him. He had been a fool.

The emperor's words broke through the rubble of his despair. "You believe Mei Li has betrayed you, Antiochus. Believe it or not, she is helping you. It is I who should be jealous."

That could not be possible. What could he mean she was helping him by betraying him? Was this some twisted eastern way of thinking?

The emperor said, "I will take you to them."

To them? What did he mean by "them?"

As if reading Antiochus' mind, he added, "To the dragons."

Antiochus remained mute, unbelieving.

The emperor added, "Fear not. There is no need for weapons."

Will he throw me to the dragon as an offering? thought Antiochus.

He had nothing to lose now. "May I bring my magus, Balthazar?"

"If it will make you feel better, you may bring him."

Really? thought Antiochus. *He would jeopardize one of his captive wise men?*

Or he was getting rid of the two foreigners most dangerous to his throne.

CHAPTER 19

The imperial carriage was accompanied by its usual caravan-entourage on a road leading toward a stone quarry just outside the city. Inside, Antiochus, Balthazar and the emperor rode in the royal comforts of silken cushions and a strange suspension system under the wheels that afforded them a soft ride. A palace guard of twenty followed them discreetly at a distance. But what concerned Antiochus most was that Wu Shu sat with the carriage driver up front.

Antiochus had had just enough time alone with Balthazar to discuss their options and prepare for their fate. As long as the emperor was foolish enough not to bind them, and to be so close to them, they would return his favor, by concealing daggers to cut his throat the second they opened the door to an armed Wu Shu awaiting them. Antiochus was an expert with weapons himself, but without a comparable sword in his hand, he knew he didn't stand a chance against the emperor's champion.

It made sense to Antiochus that they would be executed quietly outside the city, where Mei Li could not protest and they could not call upon their other magi for help.

Balthazar had made the mad suggestion to take the emperor hostage, but to what hope? They were in the heart of the East, thousands of miles from home. It was a dragon that their king wanted, and the emperor was now bringing them to that beast, as they had asked.

The emperor stared at Antiochus as if he knew his thoughts. "This bastard son of the king that you spoke of, do you think that if that son were to have a dragon, it would gain him the approval of the people?"

Antiochus stared back. The emperor knew his secret. He had to. Antiochus responded in kind, "Does a dragon gain an *emperor* the approval of the people?"

Huang Di smiled. "No. For if the people were to discover that their emperor was the son of, say, a servant in the kingdom, rather than the emperor's own seed, no dragon would be large enough to help him exercise the power he needed to rule. That is why such an emperor would never reveal his true identity and origin."

Antiochus thought the analogy sounded too personal to the emperor, as if he were implying it of himself. Was this what Mei Li had meant when she said that Antiochus had more in common with the emperor than he realized? Could this be his own secret offered as an act of diplomacy? Ch'in Shih Huang Di was a bastard son as well?

The emperor concluded, "Dragons die as do emperors. A ruler can only reign through fear for so long before that fear crumbles beneath the weight of the people."

Balthazar now spoke up, "Power must be given, it cannot be taken."

The emperor smiled at him—like a snake. Balthazar feared he may have been too bold in his declaration to this tyrant.

"Ah," said the emperor. "But power can only come from the living, not the dead."

What did that mean? Was Antiochus' fear justified? Was the emperor hinting at his own quest for immortality or at some nefarious intent for his captives? Antiochus tensed up again, in anticipation of their fate.

The carriage halted and the door opened for them. Antiochus placed his hand near his blade. Balthazar moved closer to the emperor for the opportunity of a quick grip.

Wu Shu awaited them. But he was not armed for the kill. There was no squad of assassins to surprise them. They didn't need a squad with Wu Shu there.

The emperor stepped out of the carriage first, and looked with amusement on the fearful looks of his two Greek guests. "What were you expecting, my visitors? A dragon to jump out at you?"

He laughed maniacally. Like a madman. And then he stopped and held his head in pain. He stumbled to gain his footing. Balthazar had jumped out and held up the faltering ruler. Then the emperor vomited into the grass and weeds.

"Sometimes I think my scholars are feeding me poison to make me go mad instead of immortal."

He had no idea how right his sardonic comment actually was. Balthazar was not about to tell him what quicksilver and arsenic do to the human body. But he thought, *A madman may prove far harder to contain.*

The emperor and Wu Shu led them down a path off the road. He told them, "This is where I excavate stones for my monuments around the empire. You saw one of them at Langya when you arrived."

They walked down an incline into the ravine. Wu Shu stayed behind.

No rocks to hide troops. No archers above. Just what did the emperor have up his wide plunging sleeves?

And then he saw it.

The emperor said, "Behold, the dragons you seek."

Antiochus and Balthazar stood dumbfounded. They were on an elevated ridge. Below them was an excavation of rocks. They saw the bones of several large creatures embedded in the rocks, buried alive in a landslide of the deep past. They had been partially uncovered but allowed to remain in their frozen graves of stone.

The emperor said, "The only dragons in the land are dead ones. Died out generations before my ancestors. I found more in other locations. The one on the left is a griffon."

To them, the "griffon" looked like a lion the size of an elephant, but with three horns coming out of its forehead and solid mane. The one above it was a different kind of dragon, the size of a small house. In life, it must have stood upright on two large hind legs, with small front arms, and a mouth full of ravenous looking teeth. A third one looked like a huge bat, but with a strange head like a crocodile and a wingspan of at least thirty feet.

These articulated remains could truly be the strangest thing Antiochus had seen in this entire land of exotic mysteries.

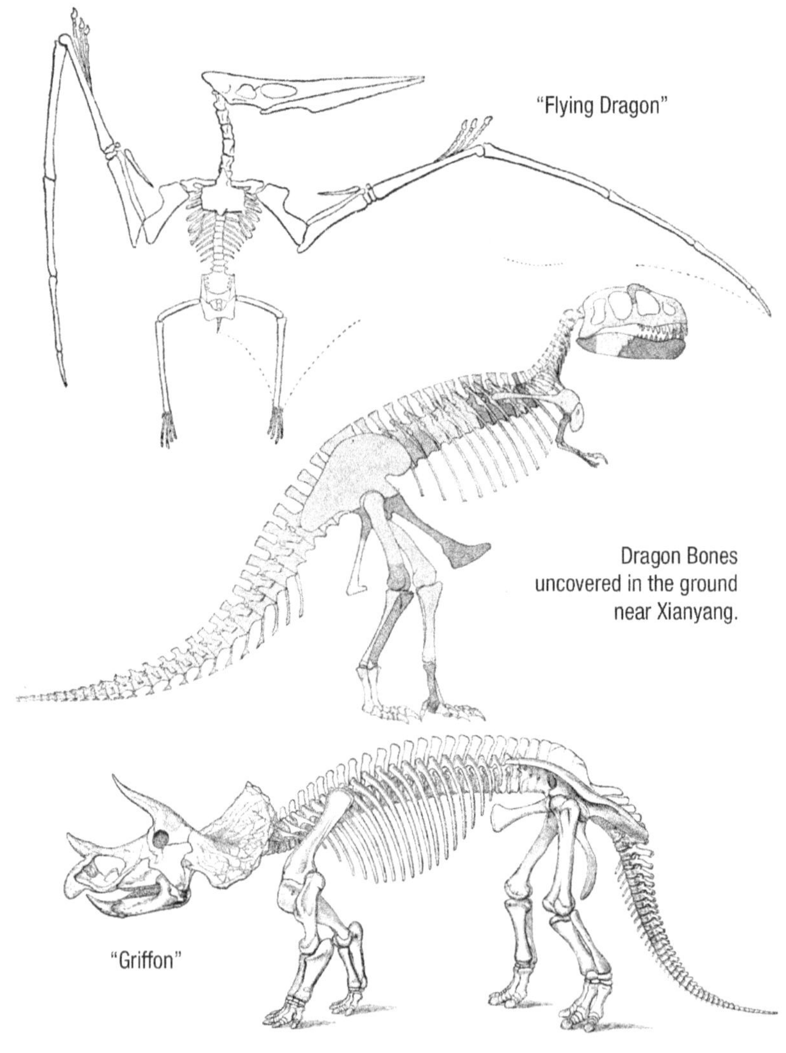

The emperor said, "Stories of dragons are mere legends of thunder lizards in primeval days. There are no living dragons in Tianxia."

Antiochus and Balthazar stared in frozen wonder at the bones of the long dead monsters of a distant age.

This changes everything, thought Antiochus. *Everything. And not for the better.*

On their way back to the carriage, they were met by Meng Tian and Li Ssu arriving in a huff on their horses, followed by their wards, Fusu and Huhai.

They both jumped off their mounts and bowed to the emperor. Li Ssu took the lead. "With respect, my emperor, we must speak immediately."

The emperor looked at Antiochus and Balthazar with a guilty tight-lipped look as a child would give when caught stealing honey cakes.

He said to them, "Will you please forgive my impatient chancellor and insistent general their intrusiveness. This will be but a moment."

Antiochus and Balthazar bowed in deference.

The emperor added, "My sons, wait here and entertain our guests with Wu Shu." Fusu and Huhai bowed ceremoniously, but with looks of incredulity.

The three Ch'inese leaders entered the carriage and shut the door.

They needn't have bothered, because the thin walls hardly obstructed their discussion from the ears of the Seleucid eavesdroppers and their royal family company.

Li Ssu's voice was incredulous. "Your majesty, is it true that you have sent the chief magician Xu Fu on yet another extravagant sea expedition to search for the Islands of the Immortals?"

Huang Di must have nodded because Li Ssu continued. "I have been warning you for months that the treasury is dangerously depleted from your pursuits of this elixir of immortality."

Meng Tian's booming voice added, "And the building of the Long Wall."

The emperor said, "Ah, the Wall."

Antiochus and Balthazar had heard that the Long Wall was a three thousand mile long barrier along the outer edge of the empire. It was a pet project of a determined tyrant who would not consider the financial consequences of his actions.

Meng Tian said, "There are reports of giants amassing north of Yanjing.

Antiochus and Balthazar shared a look of fear.

The emperor said, "Do not worry about the giants."

Li Ssu complained, "The economy is collapsing. The people are starving. Your majesty, with humble respect, this quest for immortality cannot continue. You have sons that will ensure dynasty."

Antiochus saw Fusu and Huhai fidget nervously. They were both unqualified to lead the empire, and they no doubt knew they were dispensable if the emperor achieved eternal life.

This must be truly serious, for Antiochus had not heard Li Ssu and Meng Tian agree on anything the entire time he had been here. The two always seemed at odds with one another.

Meng Tian said, "I have heard murmurs of mutiny among the soldiers' ranks."

The emperor's response was instant. "Kill all the mutineers and their families."

Meng Tian said, "But an uprising of the nomadic laborers has already begun near Yanjing in the far north. Rumors are as many as twenty thousand men."

"Then take an army of forty thousand, go to the wall and crush it, General."

"It will not be easy, my lord. It is six hundred miles to the site of the insurrection. It will take a force of forty thousand soldiers a fortnight's rapid march at least. The rebels are entrenched and have been building their numbers for some time. They will be organized for defense by the time I arrive."

The emperor's voice seemed to turn into a soothing, motherly calm. "Fear not, my mighty general. I will send you the help you need for both insurrection and giants."

Antiochus and Balthazar looked askance at one another. What help was he talking about? More troops? Secret weapons? For all the depraved leader's degenerating behavior, when he spoke of his "help," he seemed to suddenly be taken by an unnatural calm.

What was this mad man hiding? Antiochus could not help but think that Mei Li had something to do with it. Her subterfuge, her betrayal. What was she after?

But then the emperor said, "And General, take my sons with you to the Wall."

The Greeks saw Huhai cringe in dread of his duty. Fusu was not so fearful.

Meng Tian said, "Your highness, what of the danger?"

The emperor said, "If they do not go, they will never gain the experience they need to lead the imperial army. And if they die young in battle, then they were not qualified by fate to be emperor."

Both the sons now appeared frightened by their future.

Li Ssu interrupted. "Your highness, may I recommend, you hold back Huhai. I am in the middle of important legal teaching with him, and I cannot afford such disruption for his education."

Huang Di knew that the key to continuing the Legalist transformation that he had begun was a thorough indoctrination in its principles.

He said, "Granted. General, take Fusu alone. I am tired of Fusu blathering on about Confucians and their ancient traditions. Let him see how these friends of his defy law and order."

Huhai's fear turned to a subtle smirk. Fusu frowned with disappointment.

Antiochus and Balthazar now knew exactly how each of the imperial advisors were jockeying for influence with the royal family. The machinations of power were the same across all kingdoms, West and East.

CHAPTER 20

Antiochus awoke to a soft sound in his bedchamber. The light of an oil lamp fell across his face in the dark of night.

With lightning speed, he was up and out of bed with his short sword aimed in the direction of his intruder.

Mei Li gasped with fright, and almost dropped the lamp.

"How did you get in here?" he said.

"Secret tunnels. Built by the emperor so he could travel unseen between locations. His fear and madness is multiplying. He suspects everyone of conspiracy."

He kept the sword to her throat. "I cannot say that I blame him."

She said, "You have been led astray by the emperor."

That was no surprise to him. But which lie was she referring to? She whispered with dread, "The bones you saw in the quarry were a decoy, to distract you from the truth that you came in search of. There *are* living dragons of Tianxia."

Antiochus couldn't believe what he had just heard. There *are* dragons in Tianxia?

He said, "You betrayed me. Why should I trust you?" The sword stayed firmly in the air.

"I did not betray you, Antiochus. I gave only enough information as was necessary to reassure him of my loyalty."

He lowered his sword. "Why did he lie to me?"

"Our people trace our roots back to the Confusion of Tongues and the Great Dispersion."

"We have a similar legend."

She explained, "The exalted temple-tower of Babel was where the Dragon first sought to unite mankind under his reign. All under heaven. But Shang Di ruined his plans by confusing the languages of nations and dispersing them upon the earth. My people left and settled here. And that is why the emperor sent his soldiers to return to the tower and kidnap your magi. He thought they might hold the secrets of the original tower and with it, immortality."

Antiochus said, "You say the Dragon is here."

She said, "He is not as you think. His name is Yu Huang. He is known as the Jade Emperor, and he is worshipped by many of my people as the supreme head of the gods."

"What does Shang Di think about that?" he remarked.

She said, "The Jade Emperor is a heavenly imposter. Because of the rebellion of Babel, Shang Di allotted all the nations under the authority of the lesser gods. Those who would not worship the creator would worship the host of heaven as idols, creatures like Yu Huang. He is the first of the Three Pure Ones."

Antiochus could not help but think of his own national deities Marduk, Ea and Ishtar. "Who are the other two?"

She said, "Mere servants of the Dragon. The emperor is going to his tower to sacrifice to them tonight. I can take you there."

"Why are you helping me?" His voice was still cold, untrusting.

She said, "I am the daughter of the high priest of Shang Di. The emperor took me by force as his concubine when the priests went into hiding."

"So that is the cause of his hesitation to kill you," said Antiochus.

"No one knows where the priests are," she said. "I want to help you capture the Dragon because it will bring back the worship of Shang Di to my people. And it will save my father's life."

His heart pounded in his chest. His head was spinning with confusion. Could he trust this woman who had already betrayed him? She had done so for her own protection. Would she not be protecting her father and the other priests in the same way? Family was the very thing that betrayed him, that condemned him to this impossible quest.

On the other hand, she was his only chance.

He said, "We have to get Balthazar."

•••••

Mei Li, Antiochus and Balthazar slipped out of the city's gates through one of the tunnels that led to the river bank. They mounted a small cutout boat and made their way across the river to a horse stable. They rode at full gallop to the emperor's temple-tower under a cloudy, moonless night.

They must have caught up with the emperor's entourage taking the river, because they could see their lights encamped at the base of the tomb, and the lights of a party ascending the stairs to the top.

Mei Li whispered, "I know another way in."

They slipped up to a non-descript area on the outskirts of the laborers' city. A hundred feet away from their concealment, a guardhouse stood beside a small incline that led down into the earth.

Mei Li said, "That is an underground entrance that will lead us to the heart of the tomb."

It looked quite a distance away from the ziggurat.

Balthazar said, "That is a long tunnel."

There were about twenty guards.

Antiochus drew his sword. "Well, Balthazar, do you feel practiced and ready to take out some soldiers? I can't do this alone."

Balthazar pulled off his satchel that was slung around his back. He said, "We don't have to. I have a better idea."

The soldiers at the guardhouse were not all alert. Some stood about, others played a board game that required concentration.

But when the magician approached them from the darkness, a whistle brought them all to attention with weapons at the ready.

A guard announced, "Halt. This is a forbidden area under the emperor's command."

But the guard himself halted when he saw that the magician in a black leather outfit and cape was a woman. A beautiful woman with a scar down her face. Even with the scar, she was bewitching. It took no time before all the men stood around her, more like enchanted monkeys under a spell than armed guards protecting an imperial tunnel.

She said, "Forgive me, mighty warriors of the emperor, but I am an apprentice magician, still perfecting my craft. Would you mind if I practice for your eyes?"

Some of them nodded their heads and shrugged with resignation. The only sensible one in the lot, an aged captain, spoke up, "You may perform a trick or two, and then be gone with you."

The spell that Balthazar had cast from hiding was only working on the younger men with their interest in the beautiful young specimen before them. The older captain must have been a eunuch.

She had to get behind the soldiers so her back would be to the tunnel entrance. But most of the men were in a semi-circle right in her way.

She said to the gawking guards, "First, I will need someone to put under a spell. Would any of you volunteer to help me?"

Most of the soldiers raised their hands, eagerly seeking to be chosen. She chose the least intimidating one, a small chubby guard who looked as if he should have been a baker. She waved him to come near with a seductive look.

The doughy soldier glanced around proudly at the others and stepped forward. He stood transfixed by her look. She told him to close his eyes and placed her hand on his face. She could feel the poor soul shiver beneath her touch.

She blew some dust in his face. She grasped a green amulet around her neck and offered an incantation. She then said to the soldiers, "What animal would you like him to transform into?"

The soldiers shouted out several animals like donkeys, mice and pigs. She said, "I have an idea. Since this is the year of the rooster in our zodiac, then let us make him a rooster." The men agreed.

She whispered into his ear.

The doughy guard started to stamp his feet, arch his back and lift up his head. He then strutted around rooster-like to the men's great amusement.

They were diverted with their laughter as she told him, "Look, there goes a hen!" She pointed out into the dark. He crowed like a cock and strutted off into the darkness after the imaginary female.

Again, the soldiers laughed.

But the old captain was not laughing. He watched Mei Li with the eye of a hawk. He was suspicious. He stepped out front and ordered some soldiers to go retrieve the enchanted chubby rooster. He said to Mei Li, "Of what use is such silliness to the emperor's magicians? He seeks immortality, not parlor games."

"My dear Captain," she replied, "you are correct." She stealthily slipped her hands in and out of her pockets. "The emperor needs serious magicians, and I take that seriously."

She slapped her gloves together and small explosions of fire burned in her hands. The soldiers' amusement turned to awe.

She walked toward them holding her fiery hands out, flames burning like she was the goddess of the underworld. "Would anyone like to hold onto this fire for me?"

The captain backed away. As she walked forward, the soldiers parted.

"Pity. All good magicians need assistants."

Her back was now to the tunnel entrance down the ridge behind her. She rubbed her hands together and the fire went out, leaving her hands smoking. Some of the soldiers clapped. The Captain was having none of it. He advanced toward Mei Li.

Mei Li then drew out a small sphere from her bag and said, "I will not take any more of your precious time this evening, dear imperial soldiers. I bid you farewell."

She dropped the small sphere to the ground and a large flash exploded, blinding their eyes momentarily. A huge puff of smoke followed the flash.

When it dissipated, she was gone. And the soldiers clapped again with amazement.

The Captain said, "You fools." He marched up to where she had been. He looked down at the entrance of the tunnel not far away with an angry frown. "You five, come with me."

They filed down to the tunnel entrance with pikes and swords ready, expecting to find their enchantress trying to get in.

But no one was around. The large gates were locked.

The Captain looked around with a torch. No sign of the female magician. He tried the gates again. They were securely locked. He led the soldiers back to their guardhouse. "No more foolishness this evening. We have a responsibility to the emperor."

Behind the locked gates of the tunnel, Mei Li hid with Balthazar and Antiochus until they heard them leave. Balthazar secreted the small metal tool he used to pick the lock.

"Well done," whispered Balthazar. "You had them licking your palm like hungry dogs."

Mei Li said, "Men are simple. Easy to distract."

She gave a naughty look to Antiochus, who said to Balthazar, "Just don't let her have any more of that magic dust."

Balthazar used some of his materials to light a torch.

When they turned around to make their way through the tunnel, the men stood still in astonishment.

Before them were ten parallel tunnels, separated by a few feet each, all running in the same direction toward the emperor's tomb. And in each one of the ten tunnels stood rows and rows of soldiers. Thousands of them, four wide and lining up deep into the tunnels before them.

But they were not living soldiers, they were clay statues. Hardened ceramic in the fires of an oven. Larger than life at about six feet tall each, standing in position facing the entrance with weapons in hand. There were even horses and chariots. They were laid out in proper military formation with their plate armor, hair knotted to the right on the tops of their heads.

But whereas in real life, the soldiers wore leather and plain colored outfits, these were painted with bright colors, covered in shiny lacquer. Purples, greens, blues and reds.

"What is this?" said Antiochus.

"It is the emperor's spirit army," she said, "prepared to protect him after he dies and is buried in his tomb."

"How many are there?" said Balthazar.

"Tens of thousands. They fill the tunnels. There are several of these pits around the tomb. The emperor wanted to replicate his entire army. He has been making them for many years."

Royalty in every nation tended to be buried with possessions and wealth in preparation for the afterlife, but Antiochus had never heard anything of this magnitude. Not even in the pyramid tombs of the great Pharaohs of Egypt.

Mei Li said, "He believes that the afterlife would require bolder soldiers for protection than in our world, so he made them larger than life and more colorful."

The purpose of such creations was rooted in the chthonic theology of the dead. Burying the real bodies of dead soldiers with the hopes of them protecting the emperor would be futile, for they would be dead and would rot into useless bones. But ceramic images of soldiers would be permanently available resources to the spirit world.

Mei Li said, "Come, we have a long way to the emperor's tower."

They could barely make it past the four-wide ceramic statues.

As they passed them, Balthazar noticed that the soldiers were not mass produced as from a template, but rather each soldier was a unique individual with a unique face. Amazing.

How godlike this emperor thought himself to be.

CHAPTER 21

Huang Di left his retinue of servants at the entrance to the white temple at the top of his tomb-tower five hundred feet above the sprawling laborer's city. He took the live goat from the priest and carried it alone in his arms into the temple.

A horned altar of stone stood in the center of the sparse functional sanctuary. There was no roof on the structure. Huang Di could see the clouds had dissipated so the moon and stars shone in the sky above. This was good.

He laid the squirming goat upon the altar and prayed silently. Then he held it firmly, took out a sacrificial dagger, and cut its throat. It made guttural gurgling sounds as it died.

He loved to see the life bleed out of creatures. The breath of life was the mysterious signature of creation by the gods. To cut, strangle or suffocate that life out of a victim was the ultimate expression of control over another being. It made him feel divine.

He let the blood of the sacrifice flow down the altar channels into the floor below, where it would drip down into the interior of the tower.

After most of the blood had poured out, he planted his feet and pushed on the altar. It was large and made of stone, but was on a leverage system that allowed him to move it without much strain. It moved like the handle of a door. A very big door.

The sound of grinding stone could be heard as the floor itself began to move.

He picked up the sacrifice in his arms and walked over to the edge of the sanctuary, grabbing one of the torches on the wall. He waited as the entire center floor dropped several feet and slid over, creating a huge opening into a hollow. In that opening were gigantic mirror devices that seemed to catch the rays of the moon and point them downward into the bowels of the tomb below.

He found a small brick stairwell and descended into the hidden interior.

• • • • •

Mei Li led Antiochus and Balthazar out of the secret tunnel entrance into the southern end of the tomb. The ziggurat interior was a vast hollow space filled with a forest jungle of trees and foliage.

Balthazar was in awe. "He has recreated a garden of the gods."

Antiochus mocked, "A paradise for a tomb."

Mei Li whispered back, "It is a replica of Tianxia."

She pointed above them to the sloped roof filled with sparkling stars like a night sky. She explained that those were large gems embedded into the brick. They were sparkling from the light that came from a large opening in the top of the tomb. Gigantic mirrors reflected the moon above down into the chamber below. A small solitary figure with a torch descended steps along the inside wall.

Mei Li whispered, "That is the emperor. He is headed to the center where the throne of the Dragon resides."

As they moved forward through the foliage, they came upon a river of liquid that flowed through the jungle. Balthazar knelt down for a closer look.

"This is quicksilver."

Antiochus said, "A river of immortality?"

Balthazar said darkly, "Do not touch it or you will die." Sticking a human hand into the liquid metal would result in it absorbing quickly into the skin and bloodstream. It would poison the internal organs and brain. The human body would react with headaches, nausea, vomiting and ultimately end in convulsions and death. It might take a few hours, but it was that deadly with significant exposure.

Mei Li said, "We must be silent."

They made their way quietly over a small bridge and into the brush.

• • • • •

Huang Di approached the central platform in the midst of the garden. It was on a raised high place with steps leading up to a horned altar in the center. He made it up the ten foot tall platform and approached the altar with the body of the goat he had brought with him. The blood from the sanctuary above had already dripped down from above and splattered on the altar before him.

Antiochus, Balthazar and Mei Li watched silently from the foliage at the perimeter of the clearing. They saw the emperor kneel down and bow his head.

The sound of splashing drew their attention to the river of quicksilver passing near their hiding place and the altar.

They saw something swimming in the metallic liquid. It was a large serpent of some kind, its scaled back rising above and sinking below the surface as it approached the altar area.

Then the creature climbed out of the river and they could see it was ten feet long. But rather than the shape of something like the bones they saw in the ravine, this was more like a long snake with small legs at the far ends of its body. It had a reptilian head, but its body was not rugged muscles and bones, it was more fluid like water. It moved with mystical smoothness, like a phantom through the air. Antiochus knew that before his eyes stood the evidence his skeptical mind had required of him. This was indeed a living, breathing Dragon.

It made its way up the platform to the altar. When it reached the top, it changed. It twisted in on itself and transformed its shape before their eyes into a humanoid figure about eight feet tall in strange royal garb and cape.

Balthazar recognized it. It was a creature that reminded him of the living presence of Marduk in his own temple at Babylon. Not the same being, but the same kind of being. Subtle scales, reptilian eyes of lapis lazuli, a subtle bronze shimmering to its skin.

It was a Shining One.

And just like Marduk, it took the goat and sank its teeth into the animal to suck whatever blood was left in it.

The emperor remained prostrate.

The Shining One stepped down from the altar to a throne of gold and jewels below. It would be the emperor's own throne had not this creature been here.

Then two other similar-looking Shining Ones materialized from the bush behind the throne to stand as silent sentries. Antiochus knew these must be the Three Pure Ones.

Pure evil, he thought.

Huang Di scrambled off the altar and knelt before the great being. He said, "Mighty Jade Emperor, Yu Huang, I worship you and offer this sacrifice to plead for your help."

When the being spoke, it sounded like many voices and sent shivers down the backs of the hidden spies. "Why do you summon me?"

Huang Di trembled in his voice, "My lord and god, a revolt has occurred at the Long Wall. I have sent my general with an army to address it, but it is already out of control. I need the power of the Dragon to quench the rebellion."

The Jade Emperor remained quiet.

Huang Di added nervously, "I have not sought your intervention since the conquest of the six kingdoms." The Dragon did not reside in Tianxia, though he made plenty of visits during key moments in its history.

The great creature said, "You are unaware that this chamber has been defiled by foreign prowlers."

Antiochus looked fearfully at Mei Li and Balthazar. They had been found out. He had to think fast.

He whispered, "Balthazar stay here."

Balthazar said, "You need me."

"Give me your magic. If I fail, stay hidden."

Balthazar refused.

They heard the voice of Yu Huang from the throne. "Or are there two of you?" He must have had preternatural hearing.

Balthazar whispered to Antiochus, "I am but your servant."

Antiochus grabbed the satchel and stepped out of the bush into the clearing. Mei Li followed him.

They saw the shocked look on the emperor's face. Enraged, he blurted out, "I will skin you both alive."

Antiochus pulled out a clay tablet from the satchel. He read the incantation, "I adjure you by the gods. May the poison and venom of my enemies, the evil of your lips and deeds return to you. May your traps and snares bind you."

The booming voice of Yu Huang interrupted his words. "You think you can bind me with an incantation? I *created those* for the Babylonians."

Antiochus noticed that Yu Huang had transformed back into the Dragon. He shimmered and again became the humanoid figure.

Mei Li threw two spheres at the feet of the divinity and the emperor. A cloud of grey dust filled the air, enveloping them both.

Antiochus moved speedily after her, using flint to light the dust cloud on fire.

The divinity moved immediately, drawing his cape out and covering the emperor in its folds–just as the cloud ignited into a wall of fire all around them.

But just as suddenly, a wall of water exploded outward from Yu Huang and drowned the flames.

Antiochus and Mei Li stepped backward in fear. The deity had transformed again into the Dragon and had wound his way up to Antiochus, glowering into his face. His eyes were reptilian and cold, his teeth, frightening. "Western fools. You cannot capture spirit with matter."

He rose up, a snake floating in the air before them. From behind the Dragon, the emperor blurted out, "She is the daughter of the high priest of Shang Di!"

The Dragon's eyes went wide. He circled them once more and stopped before Mei Li with a snarl. "You must know where the priests of Shang Di are hidden."

Mei Li would not speak. She glowered with hatred at the being. He did not frighten her any more.

The Dragon flowed around them like a ghost in the air, the ten foot long body encircling them like a living, twisting, writhing ring. It stopped encircling them and came to rest as a humanoid again. Now he was looking down at Antiochus, his thin serpentine eyes drawing the human into their darkness. Antiochus felt his very soul stripped naked and weak before the creature.

The emperor said, "Shall I torture her? Perhaps she will talk."

"No" said Yu Huang. "She will surely talk— if you torture *him*."

Balthazar wanted to jump out of hiding with sword swinging, but he held back. He knew this Shining One was powerful beyond anything he had ever encountered. More powerful than Marduk, king of the gods of Babylon.

The magus would wait for the right moment. He slinked away into the darkness and made his way back through the long dark tunnels that led them here.

CHAPTER 22

Balthazar burst through the doors of the alchemy laboratory in the Academy of Scholars, out of breath.

"Where are Melchior and Gaspar?!" The scholars and magicians stopped working on their alchemy and stared at him.

Chang met him.

"What is wrong, Balthazar?"

Melchior and Gaspar arrived.

Balthazar looked around. He saw scholars gaping at him, and he tried to calm down. He said in a low hush, "Antiochus needs our help."

Melchior asked, "Where is he?"

But before Balthazar could say, the doors of the laboratory smashed open again.

A contingent of twenty royal guards with glaives burst into the laboratory. They lined up in menacing fashion, blocking the door's exit.

Balthazar thought, *He found out. The emperor knew I was there, and now he is going to arrest me and cut off my head.*

The emperor strode in with fury, accompanied by the steely-eyed Wu Shu.

Balthazar backed up in fear.

The emperor shouted, "Where is my elixir of immortality?" He looked around the room, a madman surrounded by fools.

The scholars and magicians froze in fear, staring at the emperor. Some of them looked around questioningly. All of them were mute.

The emperor grimaced with pain and held his head. It was getting more difficult to disguise his malady. He gathered his wits and screamed out again, "Where is my elixir of immortality?!"

Chang was the one who had the liver to stand up and speak. He bluffed with utmost humility. "Your greatness, we have not found the proper formula yet. But we are close. Very close."

"You have been working for years! Why have you nothing to show me for your labors? Are you conspiring against me?!"

Chang bowed lower to the ground. "My lord, we are your loyal servants! Xu Fu has not yet returned from his expedition. And the rest of us are working many hours in constant shifts. Some of us have not slept in days."

"I am sick of your excuses!" The emperor stomped up to the closest table full of scrolls and devices. He howled and heaved it over with a crash to the floor. Scrolls scattered, alchemic devices crashed and broke into pieces.

Scholars backed up reflexively.

Balthazar watched Wu Shu and the armed soldiers. They awaited commands to attack.

The emperor suddenly became calm. His madness left him. He looked over all the scholars in the room and said with a cool, reptilian repose, "If you do not produce the elixir for me by week's end, you will all die."

Then he turned and left the room with Wu Shu and some of the soldiers. A squad of a dozen stayed guarding the door. No one was going to get out until they were finished.

Chang looked darkly at his western magi friends.

A scholar in the back of the room said, "We are no closer than we were when we started."

Chang whispered, "We are all going to die."

CHAPTER 23

The sound of screams echoed through the stone hallways of a dungeon beneath the palace grounds. The emperor engaged in all the fine arts of torture available to the Ch'inese. *Ling chi* was the most popular. It meant "death by a thousand cuts." Extremely sharp knives were used to make tiny non-deadly incisions all over the body, making sure not to bleed the victim too much so that they would stay alive as long as possible to experience a maximum of pain from a thousand tiny cuts.

There was of course, flaying, the art of peeling a man's skin from his body and pouring salt on his exposed flesh. But one of the most creative and distinctly indigenous was the bamboo torture. Bamboo grew rapidly, like a weed, sometimes as much as three feet in a day. So victims would be tied down over a group of newly planted bamboo shoots whose tops were cut sharp. As the bamboo grew, it would slowly penetrate the flesh and grow through the body of the victim, causing a slow increase of extreme pain.

The torturer had decided to go back to basics with Antiochus. He was spread out on a rack device, with all limbs exposed. The torturer was so opposite from the Greeks' own ugly monster back in Seleucia. Like yin and yang. It almost made Antiochus smile, despite his painfully unfortunate situation.

This torturer was a small person of only three feet height, a dwarf—and a woman, not a man. *The gods work in mysterious ways,* he thought as he watched her heat a red hot iron in a small furnace of coals. She was going to perform on him the "Five Punishments of Ch'in."

The Five Punishments consisted of first tattooing the face. That one would be skipped because it had to do with the victim surviving to become a slave. The second one was more apropos. It involved cutting off the ears or nose. The third was cutting off the feet. The fourth was castration. The fifth was quartering, which meant amputating all four arms and legs from the torso. The vile little torturer was going to use the hot iron to cauterize each wound she made so that Antiochus would not bleed to death before the punishments were completed. The Five Punishments were truly an example of a fate worse than death.

And Mei Li would have to watch it all, firmly held in the grip of a soldier by the wall.

But before Antiochus was to be dismembered, he was being given one last chance. The deity Yu Huang stood over him, in the human form of the bronze Shining One. Those piercing reptilian eyes were about the only thing Antiochus had ever seen that frightened him. They were unearthly, cthonic. Superior beyond his imagination.

Yu Huang said, "The bastard son of Antiochus the Great. Trying to win your daddy's affection, are you? That is the problem with humanity. Your devotion to family blinds you to the greater fate of nations. You seek justice because you think there is some kind of higher law of the cosmos to which kings and princes are also subject. But in the end, he who reigns *makes* the laws. Because power is law. Justice can only come through power. You know this, Antiochus. You have said so yourself."

Antiochus said through gritted teeth, "How would you know what I have said?" It was not a challenge. Antiochus *had* said so. He truly did not understand how this creature, so distant from Antiochus' homeland, could possibly know such things.

"Marduk told me," said Yu Huang. "The high prince of Babylon."

The Greek word for "high prince," was *archon*.

Yu Haung continued, "Or, as he is known in Greece, Zeus." He leaned down close to Antiochus. But he was no longer cold and kingly, he had turned strangely warm and personal. "You see, we archons are legion. We have many names across many nations. Isis, Ba'al, Ishtar, Shiva, Amun-Ra. I am known in the west as Nachash."

Antiochus had heard these things before from Balthazar, but he had never taken them seriously. Now, he could not deny what was plainly, if not supernaturally, before him. Balthazar had explained to him that the word *Nachash* in Hebrew meant "serpent."

Yu Huang explained, "When Shang Di confused the tongues at Babel and divided mankind, he created the nations and their territories. Out of those, he allotted one simple people for his own inheritance, the vile people of Jacob and their despicable land of Canaan. But the other nations and their territories, he allotted to the Sons of God as an inheritance." He gestured to himself as one of those inheritors. "We are the Watchers, the principalities and powers behind the destinies of the nations."

Antiochus' mind was racing. Sons of God? Where did they come from? Why were they in rebellion against Shang Di or Yahweh, or whatever his name was, the Creator of the cosmos?

Yu Huang wasted no time. "I could do for you what I did for Huang Di. He too was an illegitimate heir to the throne, born of common seed, without royalty. I gave him the world."

So it was true. Antiochus and the emperor were both bastard sons.

Yu Huang said, "You share his seed. The blood of this people runs in your own veins, does it not?"

This divinity, this Watcher knew everything. He knew that Antiochus was a half-blood, born of Ch'in as much as Greek.

"Do you not want the world, Antiochus the Younger?"

Was Huang Di the ultimate end of Antiochus' own fate? Was he looking at the mirror image of his soul, twisted and depraved by power?

"Join me, Antiochus. Join me, and you will have your Dragon. I will accompany your return to Babylon as Emperor of the West. As Huang Di is Emperor of the East.

Antiochus knew there was an inevitable condition. A condition that he could not abide. The original temptation.

"All you have to do is obey me. Fall down and worship me and you will have the power you need to achieve all the justice you so desire. You will be a god, knowing good and evil."

The words of Balthazar came back to Antiochus, *Human power leads to tyranny and madness if it is not under the power of heaven.*

This creature and its power were not of heaven, but of hell.

Antiochus spit in the face of the great being.

The deity wiped the spittle from his cheek. "I will say this for you, son of Seleucia, you have spirit. Pity. I could have used you to great purpose." He turned to the guard holding Mei Li, who cowered under the giant's gaze. "When she is ready to talk, take her to the emperor." The guard gave a shaky nod of his head.

Antiochus looked over at the dwarf torturer with red hot poker. When he looked back, Yu Huang was gone. Disappeared into the dank air without a sound.

The dwarf climbed the steps up to Antiochus' mount and looked down upon him, holding the sizzling iron in one hand and a sharp knife in the other.

Mei Li screamed out, "No! No!"

Antiochus barked, "Do not reveal the priests, Mei Li! Or my death will have been in vain."

Mei Li struggled against her large jailer.

The dwarf laughed and spoke with her high-pitched voice, "How poetic, undying love in the face of death."

She leaned up to Antiochus' face, the knife blade perilously close to his eye, the sizzling poker, not far behind.

She moved the blade down Antiochus' face, barely a hair's width from the surface of his skin. Then over the rest of his body. He could feel the heat emanating from his instrument of pain.

"Perhaps, I should start with castration instead of the nose. It's my personal favorite."

He closed his eyes, clenched his teeth, and steeled himself for a night of great suffering.

"No matter what you see, Mei Li!"

"On the other hand," said the torturer, "I should build up to the best part. Give myself something to look forward to. Let us start with the nose." She placed the blade in preparation to cut off his nose.

Mei Li closed her eyes tightly and muttered in anguish, "Antiochus."

Pfffffft. Churnk!

The sound caused Antiochus to open his eyes.

The nose it was. But not his own. An arrow pierced the nose of the dwarf and went into her skull. She fell back to the floor like a clay statue.

Antiochus stretched his head backward to see behind him.

Balthazar stood by the entrance with bow in hand. Next to him, Chang, Melchior and Gaspar.

The guard previously holding Mei Li had been impaled against the wall with Chang's spear.

The magi released Antiochus and Mei Li from their bonds.

Mei Li said, "We must get to the priests of Shang Di."

Chang said, "Where are they?"

"They are hiding out with the rebels at the Long Wall."

Chang said, "Meng Tian is already on his way there with a force of forty thousand."

"We can beat them there," she said. "But we must leave immediately."

Chang countered, "Even if we do, they have the power of the Dragon behind them. The rebellion will be crushed."

Mei Li said, "The priests of Shang Di can stop the Dragon."

"But how?" said Chang.

She looked to Antiochus. "You must trust me in this."

She had just proven to him her ultimate loyalty in the face of the emperor and the Dragon himself.

He said, "What are we waiting for?"

Balthazar barked, "We magi are staying here."

"No," said Antiochus. "When the emperor discovers your betrayal, you will be executed."

Balthazar said, "All Ch'inese scholars and magicians are about to be executed. We must help them."

"But there is no elixir of immortality, Balthazar. What can you do?" said Antiochus.

"I do not know," said Balthazar. "But we cannot leave them." He handed Antiochus a three foot long wrapped satchel. "Give this to the high priest of Shang Di when you find him."

Antiochus opened the satchel and saw a simple primitive staff made from an almond branch.

"What is this?" said Antiochus.

Balthazar said, "It is the staff of Aaron, the high priest of Yahweh," he stopped. "If the legends are true, it is a weapon that yields an unimaginable power."

Antiochus smiled. "You are always full of surprises, magus." He wrapped it back up.

"I am but your servant," said Balthazar.

"No," said Antiochus. "You are my brother. You always have been."

They embraced as the brothers they were.

Balthazar whispered to him, "I learned of your mother's ancestry when I read the oracle bones in our archive."

Antiochus muttered back, "Why did you never speak of it?"

"The blood of Babel runs in all men's hearts, Antiochus. It is the spirit that makes us family, not race."

Mei Li watched Antiochus sigh thoughtfully.

Balthazar said, "The gods be with you, my brother."

Antiochus said, "Don't you mean, Shang Di?"

Balthazar looked at Mei Li, then back at Antiochus with a smile. "Indeed, I do. Shang Di be with you."

"And also with you," said Antiochus.

They had a mere week to travel five hundred miles or all was lost.

CHAPTER 24

Huang Di sat alone on his throne in the empty throne room. He made all the guards stay outside the palace doors. He looked out into the vast emptiness before him. Was this what it was like to be a god? He was emperor of all under heaven. He could show his humanity to no one. Not his wives, nor his concubines, nor his closest advisors. He must remain holy, separate and above them.

A wave of nausea came over him. His limbs felt weak with trembling. The symptoms were increasing. When would they subside? He could no longer stand the smell of food. He felt sick most of the time and had to go to the latrine constantly. When would he enter into a higher state of being as he was promised by his magicians and alchemists?

His skin began to itch all over his body. It felt like insects were crawling over him. He cried out in anguish and scratched himself to rid his body of the creeping sensation.

He reached down to a small gilded bronze container and opened it. Inside were specially baked cakes that were mixed with the life-giving quicksilver, arsenic and other ingredients that would preserve his body for longevity. He crammed one into his mouth and ate with desperation. He coughed and almost choked on it. He jammed another one in his mouth. But a raging migraine headache pierced his skull and he spit out the cakes all over the floor. He clutched his head tightly.

"Your majesty," came a voice at the other end of the vast hall. Haung Di looked up, trying to hide his shame.

He saw the chief Xu Fu with a squad of guards. The emperor suddenly brightened, and ignored the pain as hope filled his heart.

"Xu Fu! Returned!"

Xu Fu bowed with cupped hands.

"Come forward, come forward."

He came and stopped at fifty paces, bowing again.

"My Xu Fu has come home so quickly. Surely you have good news for me. Tell me, what did you find?"

Xu Fu bowed again, giving ample deference, showing excess humility and submission. "My lord, the emperor. I have found the three spirit mountains of the immortals in the East Sea."

Huang Di grinned widely.

"They are named Penglai, Fangzhang, and Yingzhou."

The emperor could not contain himself. "Did you meet the immortals?"

"Yes, my lord."

"Can they impart immortality?"

"Yes, my lord."

"Well, where is it?"

"It is an herb on the island of Penglai."

"Do you have it with you?"

"No, my lord."

The emperor's excitement turned sour.

"But why not?"

Xu Fu hesitated.

The emperor exploded with fury, "WHY NOT, XU FU?! WHY DO YOU NOT HAVE MY ELIXIR?!"

"Forgive me, your highness, but I never set foot on the islands. They are guarded by a gigantic sea monster to keep mortals from approaching."

The emperor's face filled with confusion as he searched within his twisted logic to find a way around it. He could not.

Xu Fu peeked up at the emperor. "Your majesty, we have crafted a very large crossbow with which to shoot the sea monster. If you but grant me one more properly funded trip, perhaps I may clear the way to the island for you."

The emperor's eyes boiled with rage. Li Ssu had been right. He should not have trusted all these charlatans with his wealth. They have consumed his treasury like a plague of locusts.

"Insects!" screamed the emperor. He felt the crawling on his skin again. "You are eating me alive!"

Xu Fu trembled with fear.

The emperor drew his ceremonial sword. Ceremonial, but still sharp enough to behead a man. "Guards!" he yelled.

In moments, Xu Fu was surrounded by four of them, ready to kill at the emperor's command.

But instead, he shouted, "Bring him to the Academy and lock him in with the scholars!"

Xu Fu breathed a sigh of relief. Until the emperor added, "I will kill them all together."

The guards dragged Xu Fu out of the throne room.

Li Ssu and the warrior Wu Shu urgently rushed past him into the throne room. The two of them had returned from checking on the prisoners in the dungeon.

The emperor waved them forward.

The chancellor and warrior stood fifty paces from the king and bowed. Li Ssu said, "Highness, the prisoners have escaped from their punishments."

Huang Di welled up with fury. "NOOOOOO!!!" He gripped a stand of a hundred candles that stood before the throne and overturned it, throwing it to the floor in a crash of wax and bronze.

He collapsed to the floor on his knees, catching his breath.

Li Ssu said, "Majesty, Wu Shu knows the concubine. He knows how she thinks. I have good reason to believe that she is taking Antiochus to the priests of Shang Di."

Wu Shu remained dutifully silent.

The emperor barked, "Find them. Find them, and kill them all!"

CHAPTER 25

Seventy miles north of the city of Yanjing, in the northern commandery of Yan, the Long Wall stretched along hundreds of miles of mountainous regions like a serpent's backbone, thirty feet high and twenty feet thick, with towers at various intervals. It had been started generations earlier, in incomplete segments built by the various provinces of the warring states. But when the emperor took command, he conscripted three hundred thousand slave laborers and convicts to repair, rebuild and extend the wall's length so that it was one continuous wall of protection from the barbarous frontier.

As Meng Tian looked down from his ridge upon the Long Wall in the distance, he could not help but think that the wall was as much a prison to keep its inhabitants in as it was a protection to keep the barbarians out. He felt this tragic conflict in his conscience because he saw first-hand the price paid by the people for the emperor's will. He was the right hand of the emperor in accomplishing that will.

He had sought to salve his conscience by influencing the emperor's son, Fusu, to understand the value of impartiality in the games of power that enveloped history. Meng Tian considered himself outside the messy world of politics. He wasn't a Confucian, but he wasn't a Legalist. One seemed tribal and divisive, the other seemed harsh and tyrannical. He dreamed of an apolitical world of law and order and getting things done. He hoped to impart those values to the emperor's next in line.

But now Fusu rode beside Meng Tian far away from the halls of power, while the younger Huhai was being manipulated in the very palace of the emperor by that cunning Li Ssu. Meng Tian could only hope to keep the elder son alive so that he might not be usurped by that treacherous tyrant of Legalism that seemed to care more about the treasury and power than his own people. The Wall was a perfect case in point.

The Wall was made of rammed earth, created by millions of baskets of dirt, wood, and rocks endlessly carried on the aching backs of undernourished peasants, morning, noon, and night. Meng Tian had pled unsuccessfully for the emperor to provide more rations. He had even petitioned for more rest for the workers, but every time, the emperor refused him. So many laborers were dying daily, that the only convenient way they could dispose of the bodies and maintain their weekly quota was to bury the dead workers into the wall itself. That was how it got the nickname "The Longest Cemetery" by the locals. Fusu had spoken up about this, but was shut down by his imperial father. At least the attempt showed hope for Fusu's future as a compassionate ruler.

Meng Tian was loyal to the throne, so he gave his advice, but he would never think of disobeying or circumventing authority. He carried out orders. He was a soldier, not a politician or a scholar. He believed in authority, law and order. Without order, chaos would destroy civilization. Had not Tianxia suffered enough under two hundred and fifty years of bloodshed and chaos of the warring states? He consoled himself with the thought that war had ceased, so the suffering of the few was the price Tianxia had to pay for the blessing of security and unity. He too suffered under commands with which he was not pleased. He too felt the sting of bad decisions by his superiors. But he obeyed his orders and gave loyalty to the emperor, the god-man of "all under heaven."

These poor fools, he thought as he looked down upon their encampment against the wall in the distant valley. *They revolt for the "rights" of all people under heaven. But they cannot even take care of themselves without the great government that provided for them from cradle to grave.* Yes, the government was corrupt and abusive, but it was also the absolute authority, so defiance against such order was defiance against nature itself.

He had learned that everyone had a station in life. Those who ruled were the few, and those who were ruled were the many. Wasn't this self-evident? His own family had served with distinction in the military for many generations and were fiercely loyal to their kings. Meng Tian was proud that he too carried on that tradition with diligence and honor. Only by accepting one's station in life could one find satisfaction and purpose in serving the greater good. It was the folly of individuals who sought higher station than they were born to, those who were ignorant and defiant of order, who were restless and caused these revolts of needless violence and destruction.

Meng Tian would return order. He would clean out the cancerous growth of insurrection and rebellion. Hopefully, Fusu would learn from him an honorable way of preserving order and authority and not capitulate to the manipulative tyranny of Li Ssu and his despotic Legalism.

Down in the valley, Meng Tian and Fusu saw a line of hundreds of Royal Ch'in soldiers impaled on poles. The insurgents had risen up and overthrown their own protectors and gathered together in the valley for their plans. They now had the royal weapons, but the weapons of hundreds would not meet the battle needs of thousands. Since these people were mostly farmers and other workers, most of them would not have swords and pikes, but hoes and pickaxes. They were not trained warriors, they were underfed peasants. Even with their passion, they could not hope to last long against the imperial army. Why would they do such a stupid thing? Why would they give up their lives for a hopeless cause? They knew nothing of how to govern themselves. They knew nothing of the art of military warfare. They only knew what they were born into. They could not protect themselves against barbarians, giants, or invading nations. It seemed foolishness to Meng Tian to prefer the cold harsh ravages of so-called "freedom" and death to the safe security of empire and life. Li Ssu abused the law through his philosophy, but in the feudal state, families and tribes were the ultimate standard, which could only result in division, disunity and endless war. With the help of the Dragon, the first emperor conquered all the warring states and brought peace and unity with his divine rule. These rebels were a mob, agents of chaos, destroyers of law and order.

As Meng Tian looked down upon the entrenchment of rebels in the valley, he thought to himself, *And when the Dragon arrives, I will kill them all.*

CHAPTER 26

"Have you ever seen the Juren?" asked a small stout guard, interrupting the storyteller. The guard was one of the nightwatch at the outskirts of the rebel camp.

Four others leaned in close to the circle in the brisk night air, their eyes unblinking, hearts pounding. They were so engrossed in the story that they neglected their responsibility of keeping watch for any spies or attack forces. They weren't trained soldiers, and did not have the discipline required for a highly tuned defense force.

Besides, the conversation was fascinating.

The storyteller continued, "I myself have never seen one, but my father—" He paused darkly. Their imaginations went wild.

The questioner asked, "Are they part of the Xiongnu barbarians?"

"No. They call their tribe a foreign word, 'Nephilim.'"

"What does it mean?" asked one of the guards.

"I don't know. My father said they are between ten and twelve feet tall, with elongated skulls. They wear almost nothing, and they travel in packs."

"Like wolves?" one of them said.

The storyteller answered, "Like mutant wolves. Their senses are extraordinary. They can hear you breathing at a thousand feet distance, they can smell you a mile away, and they can see you from ten miles."

More than one of them had stopped breathing. What was legend and what was reality?

The storyteller added, "Oh, and they can see in the dark like a tiger."

One of them looked around into the darkness. The others were too scared to move their eyes from their narrator.

"And most peculiar, they have six fingers on each hand and six toes on each foot, for a total of twenty-four fingers and toes."

One of them finally let his breath out with a huff. He had tried to hold it so as not to be heard by any giant predators. The others looked at him scoldingly.

"And they have two rows of teeth in their mouths."

"Two rows of teeth?" repeated one of them with shock. "These giants are not human."

"They are demigods, children of the Dragon. Seed of the Serpent mingled with the daughters of men," said the storyteller. "Though they are half human themselves, it doesn't stop them from eating the flesh of their human victims."

"Cannibals," one of them gasped.

A guard slipped off his rock, making everyone jump.

Then they heard a growl. They looked out in the brush. They had neglected their duty to their own danger.

Until they realized it was the growling belly of the short guard.

"I'm hungry," he said, trying to avert his shame. "I haven't eaten in days."

The storyteller broke out in laughter. The others followed suit.

Their amusement was short-lived.

A group of three dark shadow-warriors stepped out of the brush.

One watchman fell on his butt. Another peed his pants. The others lifted up their pikes.

The storyteller yelled, "Identify yourself or die!"

These bumbling farmers would, no doubt, be dead themselves in a minute.

The lead figure pulled down her hood and said, "I am Mei Li, daughter of Li Bu Hai, the high priest of Shang Di."

The storyteller guard led Mei Li, Antiochus and Chang, with their equipment cart, through the rebel camp toward the wall. They had carried only the most basic of weapons, minimal food, and some carrier pigeons.

Antiochus took care to notice the rebel fighters and their arms. They were men and boys, most too young and too old for battle. They looked exhausted and underfed in ragged clothes, without body armor. They were laborers, not warriors. They held axes, scythes and converted garden tools rather than swords and shields. Some of the imperial forces had joined them, but these were in the hundreds.

They needed thousands.

As they got closer to the wall, they passed through the village of civilians protected by the army. Women and children in groups huddled around fires outside their huts. Malnourished, sick and cold. He saw a mother holding a sickly infant. They passed a group of children trying to have some fun on the street.

Antiochus felt a deep pity. These poor wretched souls had wallowed in such squalor for so long, they didn't even know how bad they had it. The hunger had become a normal part of their daily existence.

He glanced over and saw Mei Li watching him. They shared a moment of painful empathy. These were the hidden dregs of humanity, upon which the empire was built, upon which the god-king ruled from his throne.

He wanted to vomit. He wanted to kill the god-king.

The thought occurred to him that this was not much different from Seleucia, or for that matter, from Egypt and Rome and all the world's empires. Despite their cultural differences or their distance from one another, it seemed that human nature was the same in every nation. They truly had a common heritage in Babel: the pursuit of power and immortality, and the human debris left in its wake.

The thought occurred to him with terrible truth. He had been so consumed with his own pursuit of power and glory, that he had never truly thought of the good of the people, real individual people like this, as opposed to mere abstraction. It was humanity in the abstract that was conjured to justify all kinds of totalitarian evil accomplished for the "good of the kingdom."

He made a promise to himself. He would be different if he were king. He would rule justly and fairly.

But would he really? And if it were true that heavenly principalities and powers, the Watchers, were behind the nations, why would he think he could be any less controlled by their evil schemes? Maybe the redemption he sought was not found in the affections of his earthly father after all, but rather in giving up everything he had sought for and embracing the people of his hidden heritage. He would have to surrender his delusions of grandeur and fight for a hopeless cause.

A necessary cause.

They arrived at a large tower. Antiochus looked up. It was fortified, a part of the Long Wall reinforced to withstand attack. Archers on their side lined the parapet looking down on them.

Imperial soldiers guarded the entrance—traitors to the emperor. Passwords were whispered and the gate was opened. Mei Li led Antiochus and Chang into the base of the tower.

It was not a large chamber, only enough room for about a hundred men. Seventy men in holy robes sat eating small rice rations. They looked up from their mats.

Mei Li whispered to Antiochus, "The priests of Shang Di."

They were unimpressive to Antiochus. Not at all what he expected. Humble in appearance, without regal posture or presence. He saw Chang and Mei Li smile. Hardly the kind of saviors he had anticipated for this impossible goal.

A cry came from the other side of the room, "Mei Li!"

An older Ch'inese man with white hair, full long beard, and colorful garb approached them. Antiochus knew who it was.

"Father!" yelped Mei Li and she ran to him, jumping into his arms. They hugged each other desperately. The other priests stood to attention, out of respect for their leader.

Her father held her as if he would never let her go. "I have missed you so, my daughter."

She replied tearfully, "And I, you."

He finally released her, kissed her on her forehead and looked over at her company.

She said, "Antiochus, this is Li Bu Hai, the high priest of Shang Di. Father, this is the man who rescued me and brought me here."

Antiochus gave a proper respectful bow with cupped hands. Li Bu Hai returned the gesture, then looked him up and down. "A foreigner?"

"Less than it may seem," replied Antiochus. "I am from Seleucia in the distant west. The land of Babel."

He knew that word "Babel" would say more to Li Bu Hai than anything he could express. The look of surprise on the high priest's face confirmed it.

Li Bu Hai asked suspiciously, "How is it less than it may seem?"

Mei Li jumped in, "I once heard a wise man say that the blood of Babel runs in all men's hearts." She paused thoughtfully. "And it is the spirit that unites us."

Antiochus looked curiously at her. They were the words of Balthazar.

Li Bu Hai raised his brow at his daughter and said, "Indeed." He turned back to Antiochus. "I thank you for your kindness, your courage." He looked impishly at Mei Li, "And your spirit, as my daughter so dutifully reminds me." He turned and waved over one of his soldiers, a quiet middle-aged man with a long beard, intense eyes and a brace on his right leg, an obvious war wound. "This is my general, Fan Zhou." Antiochus was impressed the man could rise to such leadership after such a wounding. "Please, will you join us on the roof of the tower?"

The five of them arrived on the roof. The archers left them alone. Antiochus could see the rebel camp before him. In the distance a few miles away, the light of fires flickered in Meng Tian's camp.

Li Bu Hai sighed as he too looked out upon the impossible odds before them.

He said, "Antiochus, I am afraid you have joined a cause you may soon regret."

Antiochus took the satchel from off his back and offered it to Li Bu Hai. "My magi told me this could be of use to you. It was taken from the people of Jacob, those chosen by Shang Di as his allotted inheritance at the Great Dispersion."

The high priest accepted the satchel as if it were a holy gift. *Perhaps it is holy,* thought Antiochus.

He unwrapped it to reveal the simple staff.

Antiochus explained, "It was the magical staff of their high priesthood. It was used to bring plagues against their enemies and other sorcery."

Li Bu Hai asked, "How does it work?"

"I am afraid I do not know."

Li Bu Hai handled the staff as a weapon. He looked closely at it. He pointed it at the wall as if to cast a spell.

Nothing happened.

He stretched it out like a talisman to the sky.

Nothing happened again.

He performed a battle form with it. He spun, twisted, twirled the staff in various positions of defense and attack.

Nothing.

It was a bit amusing. He looked like a sorcerer wielding a magical staff without any power.

Antiochus said, "My magi could never seem to get it to work either."

Li Bu Hai said wistfully, "A powerless talisman. I am afraid your efforts were wasted." He glanced at his silent general, a man of few words. He remembered something and asked Antiochus. "You say you have magi?"

"Yes."

Chang spoke up. "Your highness." He bowed. "My name is Chang Shen. I am from the emperor's academy of scholars. The foreign magi were commanded to help the royal magicians to seek the elixir of immortality for the emperor."

The high priest asked, "Have they succeeded?"

"No. Some have secretly worked against the emperor, so he is about to kill them all."

Li Bu Hai looked to Mei Li, "What of the Dragon?"

Mei Li looked away. She did not want to answer. "We have reason to believe that the Dragon is coming to aid Meng Tian's army against the rebellion."

Fan Zhou finally spoke. "So that is why they delay. They want more than a strategic defeat, they want an epic slaughter."

"Legendary," added Li Bu Hai. He stood silent for an uncomfortably long pause.

Then he said, "There is only one way to stop the Dragon."

Mei Li looked with knowing surprise at her father. "The Border Sacrifice?"

Antiochus remembered what she had told him about the Border Sacrifice, and how the priesthood of Shang Di had been abolished when the emperor came to power. It was precisely why the priests were currently exiled and hiding out in this tower on the Long Wall. The Dragon's rise to power was dependent upon the demise of Shang Di's authority over the people.

Li Bu Hai said to Antiochus, "The original Altar of Heaven is in Yanjing, just seventy miles south of here. If we can get to that altar and perform the Border Sacrifice, it will restore the priesthood of Shang Di and crush the power of the Dragon."

Their plans were interrupted by the sound of very deep and long horns from the direction of Meng Tian's camp.

OOOOOOOOOOOMMMMMMMM.

Antiochus said, "What is that?"

Chang answered him, "Our downfall."

OOOOOOOOOOOMMMMMMMM.

Li Bu Hai explained, "It is the call of the Juren beyond the wall."

Antiochus listened.

OOOOOOOOOOOMMMMMMMM.

He said, "But I thought the giants were part of the barbarian forces of chaos *against* the emperor."

Chang said, "The Juren are spawn of the Dragon. The Fallen Ones. The Dragon has arrived, and he is calling forth his offspring to serve him."

OOOOOOOOOOOMMMMMMMM.

They turned their attention from the enemy camp on their side of the Long Wall, to the dark forest on the other side. Antiochus walked over to the ledge to peer out into the black for a sign of anything.

It was frighteningly still.

A chilling roar suddenly echoed from deep in the forest. Antiochus had never heard a creature that sounded this menacing; bear, lion, or tiger. This one sounded like a bellowing demon of hell.

They watched trees in the distance shake. Large trees, a hundred feet high. It must have been some kind of tactic they used to instill fear in their victims before a battle.

Fan Zhou said somberly, "They are coming."

"We are surrounded," Li Bu Hai said. "The emperor's army before us and the Juren at our backs. The wall will not hold them for long. Fan Zhou, take over the command of our forces. We need to leave for the Altar of Heaven immediately."

Three chariots were armed to carry the high priest and his guardians. Chang mounted the chariot that carried Antiochus and Mei Li. Another held Li Bu Hai and two other priests. One of them carried a goat, chosen for the sacrifice. A third chariot was handled by three ex-imperial guards, the best of warriors.

Antiochus asked Chang, "Did you send the carrier pigeons to the Academy?"

Chang said, "Yes. I told Xu Fu everything. I don't know what good it will do them."

Mei Li said, "They need only hold off long enough for us to get to the Altar of Heaven."

Li Bu Hai heard them. "If we maintain a fast pace," he said, "we should be there by morning."

"You had better be right, priest," said Antiochus, "or everything is lost."

Li Bu Hai shook his head. "Everything is already lost. Our only hope is to trust in Shang Di for a miracle."

CHAPTER 27

All hundred scholars stood with glaring eyes at the three magi inside their alchemy lab. They looked ready to tear the foreigners apart.

Balthazar gulped. Melchior looked around in vain for a way to escape. Gaspar crinkled his face, as the familiar yet repugnant stench entered their nostrils from his gastrointestinal release. It often happened when he was fearful.

Melchior gave his brother a disappointed look. Gaspar shrugged.

Xu Fu stood before them, holding in his hand the golden jar that Balthazar had been hiding.

"You have been withholding secrets from us, Balthazar."

Balthazar said, "It is a sacred relic of our people."

Melchior threw in, "We have guarded it for decades."

Gaspar muttered, "Centuries, Melchior, not decades."

Melchior hissed back, "I meant *us*, nitwit, not the magi order."

"Enough!" yelled Xu Fu. "What is it?"

The magi looked at one another. Should they tell him? Should they jeopardize their sacred duty?

Balthazar spoke up. "A thousand years ago, the creator Yahweh, or as you call him, Shang Di, rescued a people from slavery in Egypt. He chose them as his own, and brought them to a new land for their inheritance. But before they could enter their promised land, they spent forty years in the desert wilderness."

He paused. Looked at the two others. Should he go further?

Melchior jumped in. They were in this together. "Shang Di provided his people with bread from heaven in the desert. Inside the jar is a piece of that bread."

Xu Fu was confused while looking at the sealed jar. "A thousand years ago?" He knew it would be dust by now.

Gaspar spilled the final secret. "It never rots."

Complete silence filled the room.

Xu Fu said with shaking voice, "You say it never rots?"

Gaspar repeated, "It never rots."

Xu Fu's eyes went wide, staring at the golden cup. He said, "If a person were to eat this bread, he would gain immortality?"

Melchior waved more of the gaseous smell away from his nose. Gaspar shook with fear.

Balthazar begged, "Xu Fu, please…."

Xu Fu wasn't listening to him. He said, "There would be no end to his reign of power under heaven."

Balthazar swallowed hard. "No end to the evil all the world would suffer."

It was exactly what the emperor was looking for. But it wasn't an elixir of immortality, it was bread of eternal life. If Xu Fu gave it to the emperor as he was ordered…

Xu Fu looked up at him and said, "The emperor must not eat this bread."

Those with him stood quietly in approval.

The three magi slowly realized that Xu Fu and the entire Academy of Scholars were now with them.

They looked at one another with a grin.

Xu Fu said, "You must get this manna as far away from here as possible."

Gaspar's smile broke. "But how? The door is guarded outside by a squad of soldiers who could kill us all with ease."

Xu Fu said slyly, "The front door is not the only way out. The furnaces have ventilation holes in the back that lead outside the city walls."

"The furnaces will burn us up like kindling," said Balthazar.

"Yes," smiled Xu Fu. "But you forget. We are alchemists. And in an alchemy lab we discover many things. Such as the fireproof fabric we use to protect ourselves while using the furnace. Chin!"

The crowd of scholars stepped aside and Chin approached them, dressed in a complete body suit of stiff puffy fabric that made him look like a silly human mitt or a gigantic child's play doll.

Xu Fu said, "Confucius said 'Everything has beauty. But not everyone sees it.'"

Balthazar said grinning, "Until there is a need."

•••••

A group of inconspicuous sailors boarded a small merchant junk ship at the port of Xianyang on the Wei River. It was the magi and their disguised helpers. They had climbed through the furnace and out of the city walls.

Xu Fu whispered to his three hooded passengers, "I will take you to the Islands of the Immortals. It is the safest place to keep the bread of heaven away from the emperor."

"How so?" asked Balthazar from under his hood.

Xu Fu didn't answer him. He was busy untying ropes and preparing the sails with his crew. He was busy ignoring the question.

Balthazar repeated himself, "Xu Fu, how is it the islands are the safest place?"

Xu Fu knew he could not keep it from them for long. "It is guarded by a sea monster."

Melchior said stupefied, "A sea monster?"

Gaspar said, "Would not a warship be better?"

Melchior quipped, "I suppose you'll also complain about the food on board."

"Now that you bring it up," said Gaspar, "where is the food?"

Balthazar had no time for their squabbling. "Xu Fu, if these islands are guarded by a sea monster, how is it that we will get by?"

Xu Fu said, "What other choice do we have?" He whispered some commands to his crew, as they finished their preparations for departure.

The magi could conjure no other option.

Xu Fu then said, "We have one trick up our magician's sleeve. Diversion."

"Diversion?" repeated Gaspar.

"When the emperor discovers we are gone, he will pursue us with his warship. A warship is a much larger vessel than our tiny junk. More threatening to the watchful eyes of a guardian. Such imposing presence will surely draw the attention of the sea monster—away from us and toward him."

"That is your plan?" gasped Balthazar. "Let them catch up to us and pray that the sea monster notices them first?"

Xu Fu nodded.

"Then Shang Di help us."

They pushed off silently into the moonlit night with Xu Fu at the rudder.

CHAPTER 28

The three chariots raced eastward along the wall before they turned south toward Yanjing, where the Altar of Heaven resided. They were four-horsed chariots, made of lightweight wood with two large, spoked wheels that moved speedily across the terrain.

Chang snapped the reins. Antiochus yelled to Mei Li over the din, "What if this Shang Di is not real?"

Mei Li replied disappointed, "You have seen the power of supernatural evil, yet you question a supernatural God?"

She's right, he thought. *How I hate to admit she is right.* He could not tell which was more distracting, her beauty or his own inability to see the world around him.

He didn't see the rope strung across their road. Hung between two trees at just their chest height, it blended in with the surroundings.

Antiochus and Mei Li were yanked hard off the chariot to the ground. The rope sagged lower from the impact. They caught their breaths and rolled away just in time to avoid the second chariot behind them hitting the rope.

The horses struck it full on. Their combined weight snapped the rope. The steeds plunged headlong into the dirt. The chariot flipped over them. Its priestly occupants were thrown into the air as if from a catapult.

Unlike Antiochus and Mei Li, Chang had seen the rope and ducked. He managed to stop the chariot not far ahead of the crashed chariot.

The third chariot, carrying the warriors, was able to stop. The armed soldiers got off safely.

Two assassins dressed in dark cloaks jumped out from the bushes.

Antiochus called out to Mei Li, "Are you okay?"

"Yes," she coughed. She was on the other side of the broken chariot. The priests had tumbled into the dirt ahead of them. She cried out, "Father!"

"Stay put!" yelled Antiochus and pulled out his sword. "Guards, protect the priests!"

The guards circled around to face one of the assassins approaching them, a woman with two small swords.

The other assassin approached Antiochus.

It was Wu Shu. He wielded a *guan dao*, a large blade affixed at the end of a pole like a glaive. It could cut a man in half. He spun it nimbly in his hands as if it was a six foot extension of his arm.

Antiochus engaged with the mighty warrior. He called upon all his years of training and experience as he swung his sword with lethal precision and force.

Wu Shu blocked every strike with ease. His returns were much harder for Antiochus to block and dodge. One swipe cut through his robe and drew blood. He was not at the same level as this warrior. He felt instantly that this fight would not last long. He drew his dagger as a secondary weapon in blocking the slashing blade of his enemy.

He saw out of the corner of his eye that the woman assassin took down the three soldiers in quick succession. She would be at the priests any moment.

Wu Shu's twirling glaive caught Antiochus' sword and cast it out of his hand into the darkness. Antiochus stumbled on a tree root and fell to his back on the ground.

Instantly, Wu Shu was upon him with guan dao poised to cut him through. Time slowed down for Antiochus. In a moment he would be dead.

Unexpectedly, Wu Shu froze with a grunt. A javelin pierced him from behind through his side. He dropped to his knees.

Mei Li released the javelin, horrified by what she had just done.

Wu Shu still gripped his blade.

Antiochus yelled, "Mei Li! Run!"

But she didn't run. She pulled the javelin out from the warrior's side. He grunted painfully again. She moved around him to face him. Her hands trembled, pointing the weapon at their nemesis.

Wu Shu stared at her, perplexed. Years of his unreturned love for her churned in confusion. He could not comprehend that she could do such a thing to him.

But she could.

She had been property of men like him far longer than his so-called love. This was her final freedom.

Mei Li gazed into his eyes and for a second his bewilderment vanished. His blade dropped to the ground. A mere look from this woman finished him off. He fell face first into the dirt.

Antiochus got up and pulled Mei Li toward the priests.

The female assassin killed one of the holy men with her swords. Antiochus had to get to them quickly or they would all be dead.

Chang crouched by the overturned chariot.

As the pair passed him, he grabbed Mei Li and pulled her away from Antiochus.

He put a dagger to her throat.

Antiochus stopped dead in his tracks.

The assassin killed the second of the priests.

Li Bu Hai sat on the ground against a tree. Her next target.

Chang had betrayed them. He must have used the birds to inform Wu Shu of their plans. He had been helping the emperor to find the priests of Shang Di all along. *He wasn't captured at the temple of Babylon, he was planted there.*

Antiochus was stuck in a fraction of time between two options. Save the high priest or save his daughter. All his mind was pulled to Li Bu Hai, all his heart to Mei Li.

Mei Li blurted out, "You must save my father!"

Of course. The high priest must survive for the Border Sacrifice to work. To crush the power of the Dragon. To stop the madness of the emperor. To save the world.

Two options. One choice. No good outcome.

He spun and threw the guan dao blade at the assassin. It struck her in the back and sliced into her with lethal force. She dropped dead at the feet of Li Bu Hai.

But her blades fell with her.

They punctured the chest of the old man.

Mei Li screamed, "NOOOOOOOOOO!" She struggled against Chang's grip.

Antiochus dropped to an exhausted knee. He looked around at the havoc and death. The priests were all dead. The high priest was dead. The goat had run off into the wilderness. There was no sacrifice.

All was lost.

Except for Mei Li. But she was about to be taken away hostage.

Antiochus got up to his feet and walked slowly and deliberately toward Chang.

The traitor pulled Mei Li to one of the chariots, and shoved her onto its platform. He lashed her hands to it. He held the dagger closer to her throat, warning Antiochus to come no closer.

Antiochus stopped. But he was not going to let this little rat get away.

The rat laughed. "You still have no idea."

Idea of what? thought Antiochus. *What is he talking about?*

Chang sheathed his knife. He picked up a ram's horn, bringing it to his mouth and then he blew it. The sound echoed off the nearby wall and through the forest around them.

Antiochus was confused.

Mei Li shouted, "Run, Antiochus! Run!"

Chang gripped the reins of the chariot and whipped the horses. He raced off into the night, leaving Antiochus in a cloud of dust.

Movement high on the wall caught Antiochus' attention. Dark shadows were climbing over the top of the wall. Giant shadows. Nephilim warriors. A squad of them. They were coming for him. And they were seconds away.

Demons from hell, he thought. No, worse. Servants of the Dragon.

He burst into action. He leapt into the other working chariot and whipped his horses to escape.

Behind him, the giant warriors, twelve of them, all ten feet tall, chased their human prey. The ground rumbled beneath their feet. They didn't need beasts of burden. They could run faster on their own.

CHAPTER 29

The emperor stood silently over the dismembered forms of three scholars on the torture racks of the dungeon below the palace. All three were dead. But before they expired—actually quite early on in the administration of the Five Punishments—they talked. All three had confirmed that Xu Fu had escaped with the three magi on a junk ship headed for the Islands of the Immortals. But when the emperor heard that they had the elixir of immortality with them, he flew into a rage and completed the punishments on the scholars himself.

Li Ssu wiped blood off the emperor's face with a towel. Huhai stood back timidly out of the way of both of them.

Huang Di stood staring into oblivion. He said in a strange calm, "These scholars have been a bane to my existence. Too often they have hidden knowledge from me. They have consistently fought against my dictates with their appeals to the ancestors and ancient wisdom. 'Confucius says this, Lao Tzu says that.' Well, *I say* they are unsightly weeds that are choking my garden."

Li Ssu said, "Your majesty, may I offer a piece of advice on gardening? Eliminating the scholars will only bring temporary relief to your frustration. After they are all gone, new ones will rise and learn from the same books and literature of the ancients. And you will have the same weeds once again. If you want to kill the weed, you must pull it out by the roots. And the root of the scholar's weed is the writing of the ancients."

The emperor looked at Li Ssu and grinned malevolently. "My dear chancellor, are you the only one in my kingdom whom I can trust?"

Huhai felt ignored, but he watched very closely the strategy and performance of his Legalist mentor. He asked, "Father, should we not immediately set chase for the traitors?"

"Let them paddle water as fast as they can," said Huang Di. "They will not outpace my warship. I have something I need to do first."

A cold wind blew through the palace grounds. The populace of Xianyang huddled together in the large open square, split by the middle walkway that led up to the palace steps.

Twenty large piles of books filled the walkway before the crowd. Twenty scholars from the academy were tied to twenty stakes on each of the piles. A mockery of their scholarship.

Nearby was a large pit dug hastily in the earth, surrounded by a company of soldiers holding pikes. They acted like a fence, obscuring what was in the pit.

High above, at the top of the steps, the emperor looked down on his people, his chancellor and his son by his side.

Li Ssu was pleased with himself at the speed with which he could compose an imperial decree with such precise legal language. He did deserve his position as the left hand of the mighty.

The chancellor unrolled the bamboo and prepared to read the emperor's decree. The acoustics of the palace area amplified sounds, thanks to the feng shui of its architectural design. The feng shui masters determined the physical and spiritual alignments of structures with the invisible forces that bound the universe.

The chancellor's voice rolled out loudly. "By imperial decree of the August Emperor, his majesty, Ch'in Shih Huang Di, who has received the Mandate from Heaven to unify all under heaven, who has distinguished black from white, who has established a single source of authority, and whose dynasty shall last ten thousand generations! Hear O black-haired people of Tianxia, in former days, this land was fragmented and in confusion because feudal rulers studied the past in order to criticize and disparage the present. Every one of them prided themselves on their private individual theories, based on a multitude of antique documents that all disagreed with one another!"

Huhai listened with particular gratitude. He was to be spared the laborious, exhausting devotion to learning the hundred philosophies that plagued the land's history. Li Ssu had imparted to him one solid comprehensive design to change the world.

Li Ssu continued, "Today, the past will be changed! Hope will rule the future! Hope in our dear and fearless leader, the emperor! Today, all records of the historians other than those of the state of Ch'in shall be burned! All copies of the poetic *Odes* and the historical *Documents*, and the writings of the hundreds of schools of philosophy shall be delivered over to the governors of every province for burning! Henceforth, anyone who discusses these ancient manuscripts and their ideas shall be executed! Anyone who uses the past to criticize the present shall be executed along with his family!"

The frigid air combined with the chilling declaration to produce an unimaginable silence in the huge crowd. It was as if they were all holding their breaths in fright.

Li Ssu concluded, "Only new wisdom produced under the emperor shall be allowed! Behold, the confirmation of the emperor's decree upon those who defied him!"

Twenty soldiers, carrying twenty torches approached the piles of books surrounding the scholars bound to their stakes. They lit the books on fire. The flames licked up the materials like kindling, quickly bursting into twenty roaring bonfires.

The flames consumed the scholars, who screamed in agony as their flesh was burned from their bodies.

Li Ssu rolled up the decree. But his job was not yet done. He gestured to the soldiers standing over the large pit. The soldiers stepped back from the edge, and the spectators finally saw what they guarded. The rest of the four hundred and fifty scholars had been bound and thrown into the pit dug right in the center of the palace grounds.

Li Ssu nodded to Huhai. The prince nervously gave the command to two hundred soldiers who proceeded to fill in the hole with dirt.

They buried the scholars alive.

Li Ssu sighed with satisfaction. He was particularly pleased with his clever calligraphic layout of the piles of burning books. Only from high above could it be seen that the layout of the piles was in the shape of the Ch'inese character for "devil."

"Devil"

The emperor said to Li Ssu, "Chancellor, arrange my speediest, most powerful warship. I have one last set of rebels to hunt down. And you will be going with us, my son." Huhai swallowed fearfully. "It is time you learn how to catch traitors."

CHAPTER 30

OOOOOOOOMMMMMMMM.

The last long horn call for the Juren echoed over the Long Wall and through the forest as archers and other soldiers in the rebel camp prepared for defense.

The morning dawn broke through the misty fog that swirled around the forest trees like wisps of dragon breath. An eerie pall of silence hung in the air.

The general of the rebels, Fan Zhou, stood on the parapet of the tower, looking out into the vast expanse of misty forest just outside the clearing before the Wall. His people had been the last to succumb to the emperor, but he never did. Though he did not like the feudal nature of perpetual war with seven kingdoms, he much preferred the solidarity of family and clan to the servitude of despotism. He would rather die free than live a slave. At least with the warring states, alliances could be made to overthrow cruel tyrants. With one man in power over all under heaven, who could stop him? An absolute monarch was a god, and in all his life, Fan Zhou never saw human nature as anything but warped and twisted. So an absolute monarch could never be trusted. An absolute monarch would always end in absolute evil.

So he stood on the parapet of a tower on the Long Wall, preparing to fight to the death against an emperor who had already been rumored to be going mad with delusion. Yes, he would rather be dead than a slave to madness. He had done his best to train and prepare his ragtag army of farmers, citizens, and straggling soldiers. They would have to fight the well-oiled machinery of the emperor's army, led by the decorated and fierce general, Meng Tian. Fan Zhou knew their slaughter would be great. But he could not tell his people. He had to inspire confidence in the face of the odds, hope for victory, no matter how impossible. If he lost the morale of the people, they wouldn't even last a day.

But first, the barbarians.

A war cry came from the forest. The first assault force broke out of the trees. It was not the giants, but a multitude of Xiongnu warriors with primitive ladders. They came with relentless fury like packs of wolves in conical helmets and bear furs.

The rebel archers released their weapons in synchronized volley. Barbarians fell in droves.

The few who reached the walls with their ladders were crushed by stones and burned by boiling oil.

A new war cry sounded, and they withdrew as suddenly as they had attacked.

Fan Zhou knew what it meant. This had merely been a sortie mission to discover the extent of their defenses.

The next attack would be worse.

·····

The chariots had been racing all night toward the city of Yanjing. Up ahead, Mei Li, tied to her chariot, could only think of one thing: how she had been kidnapped by the treacherous Chang, and was unable to give her father a proper burial. The thought of his body lying on the ground, vulnerable to the wild elements, made her sick to her stomach.

A distance behind them, Antiochus rode with relentless determination. He could see his horses lathering heavily and slowing down. They might not catch up to Chang before they collapsed from exhaustion.

Antiochus glanced back. The giants were not far behind. They were catching up to their human prey as they ran on foot through the wilderness and meadows of the province.

One of the strongest of the giant warriors came within sight of Antiochus. He had been closing the distance all night, pacing himself so as not to over-exert. He was not merely the most agile of the Juren, but the cleverest. Antiochus did not look forward to facing this monster in a battle.

The giant's presence spooked the horses. Their fright kept their pace racing down the bumpy road.

Antiochus could finally see the giant's features in the morning light as he drew within fifty feet. He wore animal skins for a loin cloth and on his feet. His scimitar sword was strapped to his back.

Forty feet. He had grey skin and long red hair on an elongated head.

Thirty feet. His bare muscles bulged as he ran, not an ounce of fat. Antiochus could only think of a rhinoceros; primal, brutal, unstoppable.

Ten feet away. His eyes were reptilian, cold, calculating, soulless.

The city of Yanjing was within sight. Antiochus kept glancing back at the giant. He could see that the thing was close enough to jump. When he did, it would be all over for Antiochus. He would never be able to save Mei Li from Chang. Even if he slew this giant, he would be facing the other eleven alone.

He had to shake this one. But he had nothing with him.

Except a single javelin.

Too late. The giant leapt into the air.

Antiochus pulled the javelin, turned and shoved it in the right direction.

Two huge six-fingered hands opened to grab the chariot.

The javelin pierced the giant's skull.

His wide eyes turned inward.

His dead hands hit the chariot back and bounced off, as the giant landed in a cloud of dust on the road.

This race did not go to the fastest horse, nor this fight to the strongest.

Antiochus pounded onward, without slackening his pace, and without losing the other eleven giants still hot on his trail.

CHAPTER 31

Fan Zhou saw that the emperor's forces, led by Meng Tian, were not amassing against the rebels yet. This was good. Because should they be attacked on both fronts, the rebels could not hold the line for long.

He looked back out onto the barbarian side. Stillness again. Dead bodies littered the ground.

A large tree trunk came flying like a javelin from the forest. It hit the wall with a thud, crumbling a layer of bricks where it connected.

The Wall shuddered at Fan Zhou's feet. He lost his balance. When he got up, he saw a boulder flying in the air. It hit the wall.

KABOOM.

And then another. KABOOM. And another. KABOOM.

These large stones were not launched by catapults. They were being thrown by giants.

One hit Fan Zhou's tower and he felt a part of the structure collapse beneath his feet.

A slew of archers were wiped out by a boulder hitting one of the parapets of the Wall. If they kept this up, they could disintegrate the brick and packed-earth structure in hours.

But the enemy didn't have the patience.

An entire squad of giants rushed the walls. Some of them carried trees as battering rams. Others carried clubs and swords.

A tree trunk battered the wall and created a large pit, with outer bricks crumbling to the ground.

Another surge and a deeper hole.

Crossbows and boiling oil from above deterred the monsters from getting any further. But the defenders could not last forever.

Then the general heard the sound of war trumpets from the camp of Meng Tian. He knew the nightmare he dreaded was about to become real.

•••••

The trio of magi had fallen asleep in the hold of their ship. Balthazar and Melchior awakened to Gaspar looking out a small opening. "Brothers! I can see islands on the horizon. Three of them. We have made it to the Islands of the Immortals! Which is a good thing, because I am famished, and I am dying for a good meal."

Melchior said, "Gaspar, you may be dying *as* a meal if the sea monster shows up."

Gaspar turned to Melchior with a strange look of peace and a total lack of hostility toward him. It was the first time Melchior had ever seen this. He thought something was wrong with his brother.

"Melchior," said Gaspar, "I am sorry for battling with you over the high priesthood. You are my older brother, you are much more disciplined than I, you are wiser and more philosophical. I think you would make a fine high priest. And I would have been proud to serve under your authority."

Melchior was stunned. He didn't know what to say. Only one thought came to his mind.

"Are you dying?"

Gaspar laughed. "No, I am not dying. But we will certainly all die if the emperor catches us before we make it to the islands."

Melchior melted. "Gaspar, you are a sensitive soul. And a *good* man. You are more compassionate than I could ever be. It is you who deserved to be the high priest, not me."

"Brother," said Gaspar.

"I insist," said Melchior.

Balthazar smiled. Even when these two tried to surrender to each other, they competed for humility.

Then something struck Balthazar. He felt for the golden jar under his woolen sack and pulled it out. Something didn't seem right. He jumped up and looked out a small slotted window to gauge their location. "Why are we not sailing toward the islands?"

Melchior called out, "Xu Fu? Xu Fu!"

They all filed up onto the deck and stood beside Xu Fu. Their mouths gaped at the sight of the huge warship that towered over them. It was five times the size of their little junk, studded in bronze armor. Archers stood with bows poised to launch. Emperor Ch'in Shih Huang

Di stood on the prow glaring down at them, his son Huhai and his chancellor Li Ssu stoically beside him.

Gaspar said, "Is this the sea monster guarding the islands?"

Melchior gave him a snide look.

A large bronze grappling hook hit the deck, crunching into the wood. They felt the junk jerk as it was drawn toward the mammoth warship.

"Brothers," said Balthazar. "Protect the manna!" He pulled the other two with him back down into the hold. They stumbled through the tight space and locked the hatch.

They heard the sounds of soldiers' feet boarding their little vessel above. Killing the sailors on deck.

Balthazar held the golden jar tightly.

The impact of soldiers battering the door rattled them to the bone with each pounding.

Balthazar said, "This is it, brothers. We failed to protect the relics."

The other two were dead sober.

"Shang Di, help us," said Melchior.

The hatch started to splinter open. The soldiers would be upon them in moments.

Gaspar said, "There is only one way to keep the emperor from eating the manna."

Balthazar saw Gaspar looking hungrily at the golden cup. He put it behind his back, away from his greedy eyes. "Blasphemy! You would eat of such power and become the very monster we flee?"

Melchior suddenly whipped his head around toward Gaspar with realization.

The door splintered some more. They were almost inside.

Gaspar said, "Balthazar, your lack of faith in man's power has become a lack of faith in God's power."

Melchior's eyes were wide open with realization. "He's right, Balthazar. For once and only once in my brother's life, is he actually right."

Now it was Gaspar's turn to roll his eyes.

"Can't you see? Shang Di has chosen us."

The soldiers smashed a hole through the hatch. The first one started to wedge his way inward.

Balthazar lifted up the small cup to heaven.

Melchior prayed. "Almighty Shang Di, we do this in your memory and for your glory."

Balthazar added, "We are but your servants." He opened the lid of the golden jar.

At that very moment, outside the little ship, a huge tail broke the surface of the water. It was ten times the size of the junk, rippled with muscle and covered with impenetrable scales.

It arced out of the water and slammed down toward the warship. But the little vessel was in the way. The tail missed the warship and hit the junk instead, crushing it and shattering it into a million splinters. In an instant, the junk vessel was wiped from the face of the deep.

A huge wave of sea water drenched the warship.

So a sea monster *was* guarding the islands after all.

A monstrous Leviathan.

CHAPTER 32

The giants pounded down the brick and dirt fortification near Fan Zhou's vantage point on the barbarian side of the Wall. He turned and looked out onto the Ch'in side and saw Meng Tian's army amassing for war. He blew his own horn to call his battered forces to meet them on the battlefield. He joined them from his crumbling tower.

When he arrived at the battle front, Fan Zhou rode along the front lines on his steed. The fearful eyes of the rebels followed him.

Behind him, the giants and barbarians battered down the Wall. Before him, the emperor's mighty army prepared for attack. He knew he was facing his own destruction. He saw Meng Tian and the emperor's son Fusu astride their warhorses on the top of the ridge. Beside them were not one, but four eight-foot tall unearthly looking warriors with an unearthly repose. They seemed to glitter bronze-like in the sun. Shining Ones.

He shouted as loud as he could for all to hear. "Men of Tianxia! Who are you, I ask? Why are you here this day? You are the poor and the wretched, the dregs of this world beneath the thumb of power!"

This did not sound like it was going to be very upbeat to many of the rebels who were already having a hard time finding courage.

"You are farmers, servants, slaves of the emperor! You are not trained soldiers! Yet, here you stand with me to face the very wrath of the emperor of all under heaven! You have become imperial traitors, all of you! And why?! I will tell you why! You fight because you know in your souls that there is an emperor enthroned *in* heaven, not *under* heaven. And his mandate grants life and station to all! Our earthly emperor has defied that mandate, and exalted his throne above the stars of God! You were not born slaves! You were *made* slaves! You do not rebel against the emperor on earth. *He* has rebelled against the emperor of heaven! You are not slaves of Huang Di! You are warriors of Shang Di!"

The rebels cheered with one voice. Weakened hearts found strength. Frightened eyes grew steely with determination. Doubts became faith. They had found deep within the courage to face the impossible, to fight to the death, to sacrifice their lives for their families, for their God. It is why they had come. It is why they would stay.

Fan Zhou heard the war horns of Meng Tian resound across the valley. He countered with his own. And the two armies raced to meet each other in the valley of decision.

Then Fan Zhou saw the four Shining Ones beside the general mutate and alter their shape as the armies spread out onto the battlefield with raging fury.

They transformed into dragons.

•••••

The giants were almost upon Antiochus. His horses were faltering. He continued to follow the tracks of Chang's chariot. He had to catch him. He had to save Mei Li.

He crested a hill and saw below him the gigantic Altar of Heaven in the middle of the huge area. It was twice as large as the one he had visited with Mei Li, but it was laid out in the same design. About a mile square with a circular altar in the center that rose in several levels up to heaven. Most of it was overgrown with vegetation from lack of use.

As his chariot plunged downhill, his thoughts raced ahead. Why would Chang bring her here? Why would he go to the very place the priests had been seeking? It didn't make sense to him.

Then he saw the figure of a man carrying a small woman's body up the stairs of the circular altar.

Chang.

Mei Li!

His attention had been so diverted that he failed to see the chariot stopped in the middle of the path before him.

He yanked the reins to the left. The horses turned hard.

The chariot slid behind them.

It smashed into the other vehicle. Antiochus went flying up and over it into the dirt, landing hard on his shoulder.

He rolled to a stop, coughing and protecting his wounded side.

By the time he gathered his wits and got up off the ground, the eleven monstrosities were pounding a path toward him, a mere fifty feet away.

They had murder in their reptilian eyes.

He struggled up to his feet and attempted to run. He could only limp. His ankle had also been sprained in the fall.

He heard the chariot behind him crashing aside with the force of the unstoppable giants. He could hear their huffing as he broke into the clearing near the wall of the Altar of Heaven.

Where is a gate? Where is a gate?

He spotted one and limped toward it.

He broke through the open gate into the vast grounds and ran toward the altar.

He hadn't gotten ten feet before he tripped and fell on his sprained ankle. He crashed to the ground. The sting of pain shot through his wounded shoulder.

The giants are upon me, he thought, and turned to face his killers.

He was shocked to see them standing at the gate. Or at least one of them stood there, just outside the opening as if he could not enter without permission.

Antiochus looked around.

He saw another gate down the way, with another giant standing ready and unable to enter. He saw the other monsters running to take their places at other gates. They were surrounding him. Surrounding the Altar of Heaven.

But why did they stop? Why did they not enter?

Unless they could not enter. Unless something unseen was not allowing them in. Could it be primeval magic? Hidden Watchers?

He blurted out, "Mei Li!" and struggled to his feet. He hobbled over to the circular structure at the center of the huge spiritual complex.

The ugly sound of a giant groaning in pain made him turn his head just as he reached the first level of the altar.

He saw one of the giants fallen dead at the gate.

The figure of Wu Shu stepped over the body and made his way toward the altar. He saw a bloody cloth wrapped around the assassin's torso where Mei Li had speared him. He must have followed Antiochus here on one of the original chariot horses.

He was making headway toward Antiochus.

Antiochus stumbled up the steps in agonizing pain. But a sudden surge of strength filled his body. He pushed on.

At the top, he looked back and saw the wounded Wu Shu making his way up the stairs. He looked ahead and saw Mei Li tied to the horned altar stone, with Chang Shen over her, picking up a sharp stone.

Another flood of realization filled Antiochus.

So that was it. Sacrifice. Human sacrifice to the Dragon on Shang Di's own altar. The Dragon wins.

"Not as I live," he grunted, and ran toward the altar, lightning pain with every limping step.

CHAPTER 33

The forces of empire clashed with the forces of rebellion on the field of slaughter before the Long Wall of death.

The giants broke through the Wall. It would only be a matter of minutes before the archers on the ledge were overwhelmed and walls crumbled to the ground in defeat.

Fan Zhou looked out upon his humble forces armed with few weapons, little armor, and, mostly, converted garden tools. He saw them rise up with unbelievable courage against the arrogant forces of tyranny.

But then he saw the dragons.

The four of them were each ten foot long serpents. They glided through the air and around the soldiers like free flowing water. Their spiked backs and sharp claws slashed through their opponents by the dozens. Their fangs pierced armor and impaled their enemies.

Fan Zhou knew it would be mere minutes before his pathetic army of peasants was crushed between the dragon army at their throats and their serpentine spawn at their backs.

He spotted the royal son, Fusu, drift apart from the protective General Meng Tian. He decided to make one last act of honor. He launched his horse toward the successor of the Ch'in throne.

•••••

Antiochus hit Chang in a running leap. The two of them tumbled to the ground, struggling for control of the sharp piece of flint in Chang's hand.

Antiochus' entire left side and arm were almost worthless from the wound he had sustained in his fall. He felt as if he were one handed.

Chang was a scholar, not a warrior. But he was possessed by a demonic passion. He apparently had all his body strength and weight to put behind him. He held Antiochus down and pushed the flint blade toward his face.

Antiochus pushed back, grunting in pain. He felt his left side unwinding. The flint hovered over his eye.

But his battle wits were still strong. At the last moment, he dodged his head to the left. The stone flint went deep into his strong shoulder. He yelled in great pain, losing strength in both arms.

Chang withdrew the flint and raised it above his head with a diabolical grin, ready to plunge again.

The tip of a javelin pierced him from behind. His eyes froze in shock.

Antiochus rolled away.

Chang fell to his face, dead.

Antiochus lay on his back. He was too weak. He had lost the use of both his arms.

Wu Shu stumbled up to him.

Antiochus could tell that his assassin had lost too much blood. He was pale, delirious and could barely stand. He withdrew a dagger and held it in his trembling hand.

Antiochus waited for the final blow from his enemy.

It never came. Wu Shu just stared at him and gave a slight nod. The kind a warrior may give to another in praise of his fighting skills.

Instead of killing him, Wu Shu walked over to Mei Li.

Mei Li! thought Antiochus. He was supposed to kill Mei Li. That was his truest revenge, against the one who spurned him!

Antiochus tried to raise himself up. Worthless arms would not stop him now.

Wu Shu held the dagger toward her.

He stepped up to her.

She struggled with her restraints. She looked into his eyes.

Antiochus crawled toward the assassin. He cried out, "No! No!"

Wu Shu bent down and kissed her softly on the forehead.

Mei Li could see his eyes filled with joy, not at the pain of regret or unrequited love, but with the knowledge of one final act of redemption.

He placed the dagger at the ropes around her and cut them off.

Then he dropped to the ground, dead.

Antiochus picked himself up as Mei Li got off the stone. Every movement was agony for the Greek warrior.

He said to her, "What do we do now? We have no sacrifice to stop the Dragon."

Mei Li looked over to the thicket that had grown near the edge of the altar over the years. A small lamb was caught in the branches. It wriggled to try to get free.

Mei Li said, "Shang Di has provided a sacrifice."

They retrieved the lamb and brought it to the altar.

They laid it on the stone. It bahed and struggled weakly.

He held it down. Thank God it was only a lamb. He wouldn't have the strength for a goat.

He gave her the flint stone.

She refused it.

He said, "You are the daughter of the high priest. You are the bloodline."

"The priesthood is male," she said. "A female cannot perform it. It would not be an acceptable sacrifice."

"Who said so?" he complained with incredulity.

"Shang Di," she replied.

How could he argue with God?

She reiterated, "It must be a male priest."

"But I am not a priest," he said.

They had come so close. They had everything they needed for a Border Sacrifice except the proper means for making it. They had crawled up to very edge of hope, but could not open the door.

CHAPTER 34

The water around the mighty warship was loaded with the splintered ruins of the junk boat that had moments before been pulverized to smithereens by the tail of the great Leviathan. The boat had completely disintegrated before the emperor's very eyes. Everyone on board had been killed. His elixir was at the bottom of the sea.

He stared into the debris-filled water. He considered making one last ditch effort of jumping into the water and taking his chances with finding the elixir before he lost his air and drowned. It was a desperate thought that even his madness would not countenance.

There was still the Islands of the Immortals.

He yelled at the top of his lungs. "Curse you, chaos monster! Curse you to hell!"

Li Ssu pointed to the water near the ship. Huhai gasped with fear.

Huang Di saw the back of Leviathan break the surface, mocking him with its ease.

Huang Di turned to Li Ssu and Huhai and said, "Help me with the bow."

They moved to the prow of the ship, where a large device stood covered by a tarpaulin. The three of them pulled the tarp off, to reveal beneath its folds a colossal mechanical crossbow the size of an elephant.

An ancient poet once wrote: Can you draw out Leviathan with a fishhook?

Huhai and Li Ssu cranked a large wheel that drew the cable back. They placed a large bolt, twice the size of a man, into place. The emperor mounted the firing mechanism.

Will he make a covenant with you to take him for your servant forever?

The body of Leviathan broke the surface again, within a short distance of the ship.

The emperor sighted his target and hit the firing pin with a mallet. The trigger released.

The bolt soared through the air towards its target.

Can you fill his skin with harpoons or his head with fishing spears?

The harpoon struck the great fish in its back, pierced the mighty scales, and plunged deep into its flesh. The grappling hook wedged into its muscle.

Lay your hands on him; remember the battle—you will not do it again!

Huang Di grinned with victory.

At that moment, the sea erupted. Three heads broke out of the water roaring. Leviathan was a monster of seven heads. And flame burst forth from them.

A flame comes forth from his mouth. In his neck abides strength, and terror dances before him.

On the prow of the warship, Huhai peed in his robe.

No one is so fierce that he dares to stir him up.

The emperor turned pale as he watched the creature dive deep.

The entire ship jolted forward as the emperor and his crew were thrown off their feet. Some tumbled off the boat into the sea. Huhai was one of them. Li Ssu dove into the water to rescue his charge.

When the emperor got back up on his feet, he saw a wake of white water before him as the sea monster dragged the half-submerged ship through the water. He rolled forward to the bow, now almost underwater. The ship's stern was high in the air.

Behind him, he leaves a shining wake.

Suddenly, the warship popped out of the water like a floating cork. There was no sign of Leviathan.

When he raises himself up the mighty are afraid.

From nowhere, the massive body of the sea monster exploded out of the water, ten stories tall. It dwarfed the warship.

It landed on the ship with all its weight, splitting the mighty vessel in half. A huge splash of water, rope, sails, and wood.

It crashes, the mighty are bewildered.

Below the surface in the midst of the wreckage, the emperor struggled to reach the surface. His foot was tangled in rope.

His heart is hard as stone.

Suddenly, the rope yanked the emperor downward.
It was the rope tied to the bolt in the body of Leviathan.
He was pulled into the depths.

Around his teeth there is terror. His strong scales are his pride.

Huang di was pulled deeper and deeper.

His body spasmed. His lungs gulped for air, but filled with water.

He died with his face frozen wide in terror.

He makes the depths boil like a pot.

Suddenly, the emperor stopped sinking.

The rope floated up beside him.

Leviathan was free.

The arrow cannot make him flee.

The emperor's body floated to the surface past sinking wreckage.

Nothing on earth is like him. A creature without fear.

The two halves of the ship sank down into the darkness.

He sees everything that is high.

The emperor's body broke the surface and floated as dead weight amidst the gently rolling waves filled with wreckage.

He is king over the sons of pride.

CHAPTER 35

Antiochus cursed the consequences and cut the throat of the lamb on the altar.

The stone drenched red as the lamb's life bled out.

Antiochus and Mei Li looked up into the sky.

Nothing.

All was still and silent.

The sound of giants roaring drew their attention to the gates of the complex.

The giants that had been held out were no longer restrained. They had walked through the gates and were surrounding the lower levels of the circular altar, with menacing growls.

Antiochus filled with confusion. "Why did it not work? Why are they able to approach?"

"Because it must be done according to Shang Di's mandate. A sacrifice offered in any other way is unholy and unacceptable. Only Shang Di's priesthood can effect true atonement." Mei Li's voice was filled with sadness.

The giants began to mount the stairs surrounding the altar.

"Wait a minute," said Antiochus. "Only Shang Di's priesthood you say?"

She nodded.

"You and I are not priests," he said. "But Aaron was."

Her face lit up with revelation. "The staff! Aaron's staff represents the priesthood!"

She ran to find the satchel that Antiochus had carried up with him. It had fallen off in their scuffle.

The giants broke the edge of the top altar level all around them. Ten monsters, ten feet tall each, growling for blood.

She found the satchel and pulled out the wooden symbol of the ancient priesthood of Shang Di's own people.

She threw it to Antiochus.

He spun around and thrust the staff down, piercing the side of the lamb on the altar.

A shock wave paralyzed the giants.

A huge hole opened in the heavens above the altar.

A swirling vortex of storm. Winds sucking upward.

Then fire came down from heaven and consumed the sacrifice, without consuming the staff or Antiochus. It broke out into ten streams of fire that burst toward the ten giants and razed their bodies, burning them to a crisp.

Those streams then gathered together and flashed northward to the city of Yanjing.

•••••

The Long Wall crumbled beneath the final pounding waves of the giants. They had broken through. They poured in through the breach like a wave of huge demonic rats. Women and children screamed and ran for cover as the giants smashed through the village on their way to ambush the rebel army in the rear.

Fusu rode victoriously on his horse, cutting down rebels left and right. The dragons were killing so many rebels that they started to retreat, only to be stopped dead in their tracks by the arrival of the giants from the Wall.

We have won, he thought. *With our dragons we will slaughter them to the last man, woman and child.*

Fusu began to feel the power of the Dragon. He began to feel as if he were one with the Dragon.

Fusu did not see the enemy general racing toward him with deadly intent, sword raised, eyes fixed. General Fan Zhou.

A moment before Fan Zhou made contact with his unknowing royal victim the general was suddenly thrown from his horse by a powerful force to his torso.

He hit the ground. A javelin stuck out from his gut. Pain overcame his entire body.

The last thing Fan Zhou felt was General Meng Tian on his horse above him, retrieving his javelin from the rebel's broken body. But the last sight he saw was the sky above him become a churning mass of fury and storm.

Suddenly, a river of supernatural fire poured out of the forest behind the imperial army and flowed through the battlefield. It came from the south with seemingly deliberate intent. It passed over the rebels but sought out imperial soldiers to drown them in flames.

The fire flowed over one of the Dragons, and the monster exploded into a burst of water and was gone. Then a second Dragon melted into the soil. A third, and fourth turned to water and evaporated.

The giants in the rear stopped dead in their tracks, like dumbfounded creatures in a trance.

Then they turned and ran away, back through the Wall and into the forest.

By the gods, thought Meng Tian, *what was happening?*

"It's Shang Di!" shouted one of the rebels. "The Border Sacrifice has worked!"

"Shang Di!" more rebels yelled. "Shang Di! Shang Di!"

And all the rebels began to chant the name of the emperor of heaven.

Meng Tian blew his war horn. What was left of the forces of the emperor of earth retreated and melted away into the landscape.

The rebels stood stunned in the silence of their victory. They had been moments away from defeat, but were now standing still, alive by the power of Shang Di. Shang Di had won them the battle.

For now.

· · · · ·

Li Ssu burst from the sea gasping for air and keeping Huhai's head above the surface so he could breathe. Huhai coughed water out of his lungs. Li Ssu draped him onto a buoyant piece of floating wreckage.

Leviathan was gone.

They had survived an encounter with the powerful sea monster and would live to tell of it. But now, the chancellor had a most important duty.

He scanned the refuse floating around him in the water. His eyes found his next treasure: a lifeboat that had escaped the fearsome attack of the sea monster. It floated loosely on the water, rocking back and forth. He retrieved the boat and helped Huhai safely into its hull.

He pulled himself in and commandeered the oars.

He circled the wreckage still searching, but this time, for something else. Something most important.

He found it. A body face down in the water.

He paddled over to it and turned it over. It was the emperor. Broken, drowned, dead.

"Father!" cried Huhai.

"Shut up, you fool, and do as I say," said Li Ssu. "Help me get him in the boat. We must bring him back for proper burial. But before we do, we must secure your right to the throne."

"What do you mean?" said Huhai, shivering in his drenched clothes. "My brother will inherit the empire. You helped my father write his will in this very ship before he died."

Li Ssu nodded in agreement. Yes, he had written the document on the way out to sea. Li Ssu had wondered why the emperor would have made such a wrong-headed choice. Now he would never know. But it didn't matter.

He said to Huhai, "That 'very ship' is in the bottom of the sea."

Huhai was slow to follow. He was always too slow to follow. Li Ssu sighed with disgust. "And the emperor is not dead yet."

Huhai narrowed his eyes with incredulity. He still did not follow. His father was clearly dead.

"He will not die until we are on the road back to Xianyang. *After* he writes his will assigning *you* as heir to the throne, with *me* as witness and scribe."

Huhai's eyes went wide. Now the fool was following. Then something occurred to him. "But Fusu will contest it. And he will have the support of the heroic General Meng Tian, no doubt his new imperial chancellor."

Li Ssu smiled malevolently. He had thought of everything.

"No, he will not. Leave that little detail to *your* imperial chancellor—your majesty, Ch'in Er Shih Huang Di."

The new name meant the second emperor of the Ch'in dynasty. Huhai liked the sound of that title for himself. He liked the sound of power.

•••••

Deep below the surface of the murky water, three dead men hung lifeless in the expanse of strewn wreckage. Rope and rigging intertwined their bodies, linking them like dead puppets in a most disastrous performance.

The magi.

Eyes closed in death. Drowned in the murderous wake of the sea dragon of chaos.

Suddenly, Balthazar's eyes popped open. Followed by Melchior's and Gaspar's.

They were alive.

They were immortal.

CHAPTER 36

The imperial forces at the Long Wall had been decimated. Cut down by a supernatural agency that struck fear into their hearts. Meng Tian and Fusu had withdrawn to their camp to count their losses, make report to the emperor, and await further instructions.

It had been ten days since their setback. Meng Tian had become restless. He shared a meal with Fusu in the imperial tent. They ate quietly, each silently considering the ramifications of everything that had happened. By now, his messenger would have delivered the news to the emperor and be on his way back with fresh reinforcements and new orders of conquest.

The general had convinced his troops that the unfortunate events of that fateful day were a fluke of nature. A chance storm of unexplainable devastation. These things happened. Hurricanes, forest fires, tornados and other storms. But they were freak occurrences that did not repeat themselves. They had just had the misfortune to be caught in the middle of an unlucky maelstrom. It was surely reasonable to believe that there was no way that such a coincidence would happen again when they regrouped and finished their campaign against the rebels.

Fusu worried about his own reputation over such a great loss. It would make his image as a leader questionable. How could he rule an empire when he couldn't win a battle against a few rebels? But then again, maybe this situation could be symbolic of a greater need to return to the wisdom of the ancients. People who are ruled by force through fear of death cannot be cowed into obedience forever, but people who are ruled by their beliefs and traditions will die for their higher cause. His father, the emperor, had rejected the past, rejected the lessons of history in the name of forging a new path for the future. He wanted to unify all of Tianxia, eliminate the hostility between the factions of tradition. But at what price? For this harmony to be achieved, all differences had to be suppressed, or more accurately, destroyed. All must be subjugated to the will and power of one man. Was not yin yang the complimentarity of contrary or opposing forces interdependent upon one another? Was their unity not in their eternal duality? But if yin was subjugated to yang, then the one was destructive of the many. If the value of the collective outweighed the value of the individual, then why was the collective ultimately ruled by a single individual? Empire itself was the negation of the yin yang principle that embodied all of creation. It seemed like madness to Fusu, madness that his own father exemplified in his impossible quest for immortality and godhood. When Fusu became emperor, he would seek to return Tianxia to a diversity within unity. To give back to the people their traditions and history.

And there was something about Shang Di that made him curious.

The rebels had credited Shang Di with their victory. He knew his father had eliminated the Border Sacrifice and criminalized the worship of Shang Di, to replace him with the Dragon and a pantheon of gods and spirits. But Fusu planned to look more into the history of Shang Di and his people. They had worshipped him for thousands of years. Perhaps here too, there was wisdom in the past that they had lost in the present. Perhaps this rejection of the foundations had resulted in the very problems that plagued the land. Perhaps the unity of Tianxia could be achieved under the power of the perfect Emperor of Heaven rather than the power of the imperfect Emperor of Earth.

· · · · ·

The town surrounding the emperor's tomb filled to bursting point with commoners and aristocracy alike in mourning. Hundreds of thousands of subjects spilled out into the surrounding countryside. The funeral for the first emperor of Tianxia was the most glorious affair many had ever seen or would see in their lives.

A long line of singers, dancers, military escort and royal carriages led the funerary processional through the streets of the town, up to the immense ziggurat tomb that had been prepared for the emperor during his entire reign.

Now, it was all fulfilling the purpose for which it was created. The long tunnels of terra cotta warriors and terra cotta palace acrobats, servants and animals were buried beneath the earth and sealed to protect and provide for the emperor in his death.

Servants carried the dead emperor on a golden carriage filled with flowers into the gateway at the bottom of the pyramid structure. They placed him in a tomb at the center of the interior garden paradise. The emperor's concubines and wives followed the train into the very heart of his royal resting place.

The designers of the structure then closed up the interior, sealing the concubines and wives alive into the burial chamber. Their weeping and cries for mercy echoed through the dark hollow, but soon faded into silence with the last of the huge stone enclosures.

Then the designers were closed in with the last of the walled gates. They knew too much of the secrets of this holy mountain.

The ziggurat towered above the people, a glorious monument to the wealth, power and achievements of Ch'in Shih Huang Di, the man who unified Tianxia and sought immortality to establish his power forever.

But Huang Di had sought in vain. He never found the elixir. He could not achieve the godhood of his delusional designs.

Ch'in Shih Huang Di was dead forever.

•••••

The messenger that Meng Tian had been waiting for had finally arrived. But it was not the message he had expected.

A contingent of one hundred heavily armed imperial guards surrounded the general's tent. General Weng entered, a fellow military leader of lesser age than the master, and hungry for his position.

"What is this madness?" said Meng Tian.

Weng said, "General Meng Tian, you are under arrest for crimes against the emperor and against his imperial will."

"What crimes?" said Meng Tian. "My father and his father, and those before him have all been loyal to the throne. My family has merited the trust of Ch'in for three generations. I have command of over three hundred thousand troops. What crime am I charged with?"

But the general would not say. He held out some vials to Meng Tian. "The emperor has allowed you an honorable death."

Meng Tian repeated, "What crime have I committed before heaven that I should die an innocent death? I demand an audience with the emperor and confirmation of this order."

"None will be given," said General Weng.

"I want to see the Crown Prince Fusu," said Meng Tian. "He will vindicate me."

General Weng nodded to a soldier, who stepped outside the tent. "Prince Fusu has been charged with crimes against the emperor as well."

Immediately, Meng Tian knew who the real culprit was behind this circus of injustice: *Li Ssu.*

The soldier returned with two men carrying the contorted rigid body of Fusu. His face was pale, his veins purple and his mouth covered with the froth of poison. They dumped him at Meng Tian's feet.

All the station of imperial majesty was nothing to a dead body. All authority, all power, all glory was gone. Never to return.

Meng Tian saw the end of everything he had believed in. He had thought he was apolitical, that he was merely a neutral instrument of the ruling power. Why? Because a soldier obeys without question. Because there was no authority above the emperor. It was the Way as he had understood it. And now, that authority had commanded him to commit suicide. He was no longer of use. It was too late for him to recognize a higher power than human rule and authority. It was too late to demand accountability to heaven if he had denied the emperor of heaven in favor of earth. Because of his neutrality, he had become a tool of tyranny. He had sought law and order at all costs, and he had purchased peace and unity at the price of truth and justice.

He took the poison from General Weng's hand.

•••••

The imperial throne room of Xianyang palace filled to overflowing with royal courtiers and aristocracy.

The resounding words echoed throughout the hall, "The emperor is dead! Long live the emperor!"

Huhai looked out upon his subjects. He wore the traditional headdress of dangling strings and stars. He shivered with the responsibility before him.

Li Ssu proclaimed to the people, "May he bring peace to all peoples united under heaven! All worship the Emperor Ch'in Er Shih Huang Di!"

Everyone bowed deeply to the ground several times.

Huhai now felt like a god before such adoration. And he had Li Ssu to thank. The chancellor had taught him and advised him every step of the way. He would be there to consult and to apply the wisdom of Legalism to bring forth a glorious progressive future for Tianxia, for this land of Ch'in.

Li Ssu smiled back at the young emperor. It was a reptilian smile, with calculating eyes.

They were eyes of the Dragon.

•••••

Antiochus stood with Mei Li on the bow of his trireme ship as it passed the port city of Langya and entered the wide open sea before them.

Mei Li watched the tall tower on the mountainside, her façade of refuge for years, fade into the distance along with her past. She would never forget who she was and where she had come from. But she would not let her past suffering ruin her future. And she knew that with Shang Di, all things were possible. She had been reborn and had found love in the arms of a man who would protect and cherish her, not use and abuse her. She had told Antiochus that his blood connection to the East mattered nothing to her. It was his goodness that she fell in love with.

Antiochus held her with strong arms. He knew they could not stay. And they could not return to his land. He had hoped that he might discover a part of his own identity that was hidden in this exotic eastern land. He thought that he might find what was missing in his western

238

world. But he only discovered that humanity is the same in all worlds, north, south, east and west. All nations came from that one primeval tower and carried a single heart of corruption with them to the ends of the earth. Balthazar was right, the pursuit of human power only leads to tyranny and madness if it is not under the power of heaven.

Antiochus and Mei Li no longer belonged in either of their worlds. They were now strangers in a strange cosmos. They were fellow citizens of a new and higher empire, whose rule fit neither East nor West, but was sovereign over all: the empire of heaven. Their true emperor was Shang Di. They could only explore the new horizon of hope that lay before them.

·····

Some are reborn to new life. Others, to return to their original calling.

To this end, three monkish figures walked their horses on the cold, flat Tibetan plateau, a thousand miles west of the empire of Ch'in.

Gaspar asked above the wind, "How much farther to Babylon?"

Melchior smirked to himself. "It is just over the next hill. We can stop when we get there."

Gaspar complained, "I am hungry."

Melchior said, "Perhaps we should ask Shang Di for some more manna?"

Balthazar shook his head with a smile. They were returning to their native land because their duty was not yet fully discharged. They had watched over the relics as they had been taught. The golden cup and the wooden staff were in a sack tied to the supplies on the back of their donkey.

But that was only one component of their order's calling. The other was to look for a sign in the stars that would herald the arrival of a very special emperor. Not an earthly ruler like the one they had just escaped, a tyrant deluded in his search for immortality and divinity. This coming emperor would be a son of Shang Di, a true god-man who would one day unite all under heaven.

If you liked this novel, get the first book in the Chronicles of the Watchers Series, *Jezebel: Harlot Queen of Israel*. (paid link)

If you liked this book, then please help me out by writing a positive review of it on Amazon here. That is one of the best ways to say thank you to me as an author. It really does help my sales and status. Thanks!
– Brian Godawa

More Books by Brian Godawa

See www.Godawa.com for more information on other books by Brian Godawa. Check out his other series below:

Chronicles of the Nephilim

Chronicles of the Nephilim is a saga that charts the rise and fall of the Nephilim giants of Genesis 6 and their place in the evil plans of the fallen angelic Sons of God called, "The Watchers." The story starts in the days of Enoch and continues on through the Bible until the arrival of the Messiah, Jesus. The prelude to Chronicles of the Apocalypse.

ChroniclesOfTheNephilim.com. (paid link)

Chronicles of the Apocalypse

Chronicles of the Apocalypse is an origin story of the most controversial book of the Bible: Revelation. An historical conspiracy thriller trilogy in first century Rome set against the backdrop of explosive spiritual warfare of Satan and his demonic Watchers. ChroniclesOfTheApocalypse.com. (paid link)

Chronicles of the Watchers

Chronicles of the Watchers is a series that charts the influence of spiritual principalities and powers over the course of human history. The kingdoms of man in service to the gods of the nations at war. Completely based on ancient historical and mythological research.

ChroniclesOfTheWatchers.com. (paid link)

Get a Free eBooklet of the Biblical & Historical Research Behind This Novel.

Limited Time Offer

FREE

Explore the Spiritual World of Ancient Lands.

If you like the novel *Qin*, you'll love discovering the biblical and historical basis for the fascinating, mind-bending story.

https://godawa.com/get-china238/

Also available for purchase in paperback.

ABOUT THE STORYTELLERS

Brian Godawa is the screenwriter for the award-winning feature film *To End All Wars*, starring Kiefer Sutherland. It was awarded the Commander in Chief Medal of Service, Honor, and Pride by the Veterans of Foreign Wars, won the first Heartland Film Festival by storm, and showcased the Cannes Film Festival Cinema for Peace.

He previously adapted to film the best-selling supernatural thriller novel *The Visitation* by author Frank Peretti for Ralph Winter (*X-Men, Wolverine*), and wrote and directed *Wall of Separation*, a PBS documentary, and *Lines That Divide*, a documentary on stem cell research.

Mr. Godawa's scripts have won multiple awards in respected screenplay competitions, and his articles on movies and philosophy have been published around the world. He has traveled around the United States teaching on movies, worldviews, and culture to colleges, churches, and community groups.

His popular book *Hollywood Worldviews: Watching Films with Wisdom and Discernment* (InterVarsity Press) is used as a textbook in schools around the country. In the top ten of biblical fiction on Amazon, his first novel series, *Chronicles of the Nephilim*, is an imaginative retelling of biblical stories of the Nephilim giants, the secret plan of the fallen Watchers, and the War of the Seed of the Serpent with the Seed of Eve. The sequel series, *Chronicles of the Apocalypse*, tells the story of the apostle John's book of Revelation, while *Chronicles of the Watchers* recounts true history through the Watcher paradigm.

Find out more about his other books, lecture tapes, and DVDs for sale at his website, www.godawa.com.

Charlie Wen has been heading design for video games, animation and film for almost 20 years. In 2001, he founded and Directed Visual Development at Sony Computer Entertainment on the game series *God of War*, and created one of the most iconic characters in video game history, Kratos. After a few years designing for films such as *Gatchaman, Thundercats, SuckerPunch, Captain Nemo*, and *Akira*,

Charlie Co-founded and was Head/Co-Head of Visual development at Marvel Studios from its infancy to *Avengers: Age of Ultron*, and *Ant Man*. He was entrusted to lead and co-lead the design and visual story moments for the main characters in the Marvel Cinematic Universe, while leading the team that defined the visual style across the Marvel Cinematic Universe, including *Thor, Captain America: the First Avenger, Ironman 3, Avengers, Thor: the Dark World, The Guardians of the Galaxy, Avengers: Age of Ultron*, and *Antman*.

Charlie had since been leading one of Riot Games future projects, and is currently in the process independently developing other stories and worlds for young adults.

GREAT OFFERS BY BRIAN GODAWA

Get More
Biblical Imagination
Sign up Online For The Godawa Chronicles

www.Godawa.com

Updates and Freebies
of the Books of Brian Godawa
Special Discounts,
Weird Bible Facts!

BLANK PAGE

BLANK PAGE